"I think my suggestion should come with a peace offering."

Aly saw the straps of her sandals dangling from his index and middle fingers. "Hmph, good thing I didn't get more comfortable."

"Mmm-hmm." Whatever interest Gage had in talking seemed to have vanished, for he suddenly pushed off the door frame and advanced.

Alythia was opening her mouth to thank him for returning her shoes. He never gave her the chance, and for the second time that day, her body reacted to the delicious sensation of his mouth on hers. Again, he began with a tentative exploration that quickly blossomed into a sensuous entwining of their tongues.

Gage withdrew from the kiss to outline the curve of her cheek, brush the sensitive skin behind her ear and trail his nose along her neck.

"Gage?"

"Mmm…"

"Do you kiss all women you know so soon after you meet them?"

He nipped at her earlobe. "Would you believe that I've forgotten every other woman I've ever met?"

"No," she gasped, still enraptured by his touch and feeling the vibration of laughter through his body.

"You really know how to hurt a man."

"It's not out of habit." Aly felt her sandals bumping her bottom when he switched them to his other hand while he held her. "So what do I have to do to get my shoes back?" she murmured against his jaw, wanting his mouth on hers.

Books by AlTonya Washington

Harlequin Kimani Romance

A Lover's Pretense
A Lover's Mask
Pride and Consequence
Rival's Desire
Hudson's Crossing
The Doctor's Private Visit
As Good as the First Time
Every Chance I Get
Private Melody
Pleasure After Hours
Texas Love Song
His Texas Touch
Provocative Territory
Provocative Passion
Trust In Us

Harlequin Kimani Romance

Remember Love
Guarded Love
Finding Love Again
Love Scheme
A Lover's Dream

ALTONYA WASHINGTON

has been a romance novelist for nine years. Her 2012 Harlequin Kimani Romance title *His Texas Touch,* second in the Lone Star Seduction series, was nominated for the RT Reviewers' Choice Award in the Best Series Romance category. The author began 2013 with her Harlequin Kimani Romance book *Provocative Territory*.

TRUST
In Us

AlTonya Washington

♦ HARLEQUIN® KIMANI™ ROMANCE

To my mom and dad, Alphonso and Carolyn Washington.
Thanks for being the leaders of the best support team
any author could ask for!

Recycling programs
for this product may
not exist in your area.

ISBN-13: 978-0-373-86351-8

TRUST IN US

Copyright © 2014 by AlTonya Washington

For questions and comments about the quality of this book please contact us
at CustomerService@Harlequin.com.

H HARLEQUIN®
™ www.Harlequin.com

Printed in U.S.A.

Dear Reader,

Thanks for curling up with my latest novel. *Trust In Us* features Gage Vincent and Alythia Duffy, and brings with it many of the reasons why I love writing romance. In addition to vibrant settings, the attraction between Gage and Alythia is greatly affected by assorted dramas that emphasize how very much this couple wants to be together.

You guys know I love my heroes, and Gage was a treat to create. Here's a little of what I shared about him in a recent blog: "When I craft that hero of mine, he's the only one... in spite of all the others who've come before him or the ones that I know will come after him. When I'm writing that guy, he's the epitome, the showstopper.... So which hero fueled *this* particular blog? His name is Gage Vincent."

I hope you'll enjoy this treat....

Toodles,

Al

Chapter 1

"It'd be real nice of you to have this all wrapped up by the time I get back."

"Now, you know I'm good, boss. But even I won't boast that I could make that happen in a couple of days."

Gage Vincent kept his eyes fixed on the open folder, which had been hoarding his attention for the past ten minutes. The response from his assistant commanded a smile that accentuated his words with imminent laughter when he finally spoke.

"Jay wants ten days, I'm giving him ten days," Gage told the young man who occupied the paper-littered sofa on the other side of the office suite.

Webb Reese's chuckle was a touch muffled behind the papers he held close to his attractive, heavily bearded face. "*You* taking a ten-day break? That'll be a first."

Gage's face held a stony yet sly expression.

In a show of defense, Webb raised his hands, sending the papers sprinkling down onto the black suede of the sofa. "Just sayin'," he sang.

Gage returned his focus to the folder, shut it and gave it a wave in Webb's direction. "Time to start earning that insane salary I'm paying you."

Webb's nod was brief. His earlier playfulness had now adopted a more solemn element. "You're really leaving it all up to me?"

Gage's lone dimple made a quick appearance when he smiled that time. "You've earned it." He watched Webb come forward to claim the file.

"This is a big deal, boss." Webb emphasized the reminder by giving the folder a deliberate shake.

"Sure is." A thick glossy brow rose with challenging intent and Gage studied his assistant of five years with a look of mock suspicion. "Have you learned nothing from your vast experience in my presence?"

Webb attempted to laugh over the tease but seemed too nervous to do so.

Taking pity, Gage pushed aside the other files that required his attention. He reared back in his desk chair while leveling a deep chocolaty-brown stare at Webb.

"I'm leaving this to you because I trust you to handle it right." Gage inclined his head slightly when he noticed Webb's eyes widen. "I have a building full of people who'd be happy to chime in with their two cents, argue against your points of view and suggest I fire you upon my return."

Webb laughed then.

The "building full of people" Gage had referred to— more specifically, the senior executive staff—were all employed by Vincent Industries and Development, or VID, as it was more affectionately known locally—in and around Charlotte, NC—nationally and internationally.

"I need someone to have my back on this, Webb." Gage was serious, which was made evident by the intermittent flash of the lighter hues in his rich gaze. "You're the only one who knows my tastes. You know what offers I think have merit and which ones I think are bullshit. In short, you won't just accept a bid based on the amount of zeroes it brings with it. You'll look at the people the bid is attached to, their backgrounds, the people attached to them and *their* backgrounds."

Webb's emerging toothy smile hinted at his appreciation of Gage's words.

"Are you saying you don't think your top circle of people will care about those things?" he asked.

"My *top circle* cares about the money they make me." Gage reared back again in the desk chair, which coordinated with the sofa and other office furnishings. "That's one reason they belong to my *top circle*—because *I* care about the money they make me.

"But I also care about the pockets that money comes from before it comes to mine," Gage shared once the round of low laughter between him and Webb subsided. "That care involves certain hands-on work that I won't be able to be a part of, as I'll be off somewhere wasting my time."

Webb's laughter then sounded abrupt. "Dang, sir, you make it sound like a hassle."

"A hassle." Gage focused on a point across his expansive office and appeared to be turning the word over in his mind as he reflected upon the observation. "It's not exactly a hassle. I just don't see the positive in bringing together the bridal party before the wedding." He shrugged, sending a ripple through the crisp fabric of the olive-green shirt he wore.

"You've known me and my gang long enough, Webb. My boys and I can find drama where none should ever exist. Mix in the bride and her gang... Well...you get the picture I'm trying to create here...."

"It could still make for less drama," Webb said, evidently adopting the role of devil's advocate. "Think of it as a chance to meet and get to know each other on a less stressful level before all the real pre-wedding festivities get under way."

"Less stressful." Sighing, Gage massaged his eyes while considering the upcoming bachelor-and-bachelorette getaway that had been suggested by the bride-to-be.

"It's also a time to get to know the bride better," Webb added while moving to collect the papers that had been strewn around the office during the course of the morning's meeting.

Resting his head back on the chair, Gage bridged his fingers and factored that element into his thinking. His oldest friend, Jayson Muns, had recently stunned his close group of friends with news of his engagement to Orchid Benjamin. The woman's background boasted old money. Old as in antebellum old, rare for an African-American family of the South, but it was what it was.

Unfortunately, Jay's black society princess had a reputation that had been earned on the wilder side. It was a reputation that Jayson seemed totally oblivious to.

"Ten days in the Caribbean..." Webb reminded him. "And I'm betting it won't be any hardship on the eyes at all to be around Ms. Benjamin and her crew. You can learn a lot about people by the friends they keep."

Webb continued his tidying—and missed Gage smiling miserably in agreement.

Myrna Fisher used her free hand to pile her shoulder-length bobbed hair into a loose dark ball atop her head. With that done, she reinserted the outfit just below her chin. She'd folded down the hanger to improve her observation in the full-length mirror.

"If I didn't know you better, I'd swear your ambition was the only thing motivating you to take this trip." Myrna barely turned her head to throw her voice across her shoulder.

Alythia Duffy snuggled deeper into the tousle of thick pillows along the head of the high-canopied bed. Her bright eyes never left the snow globe as she shifted it upside down, right-side up and back again.

"I *don't* know any better," Alythia conceded, the bulk of her attention on the rush of white confetti drifting down around a miniature replica of the Charlotte skyline.

In playful retaliation, Myrna tossed the outfit she'd been debating over. The garment landed across Aly's bare feet, which were only partially visible given all the other articles of clothing Myrna had tossed there during her rushed packing job.

"In spite of my cluelessness, ambition isn't my only reason for going." Alythia defended herself in a tone harboring a fair share of mock indignance.

"But it *is* a reason?" Myrna challenged. Silence met her query and she did an about-face toward the canopy, shooting a glare in Alythia's direction. "This *should be* the one time we all put business and all of those other obligations aside, you know?"

Undaunted, Alythia propped herself higher against the pillows. "This coming from the woman who missed her own nephew's high school graduation for a bikini fitting?"

"Oh, please, Aly…how long are y'all gonna give me grief over that?" Myrna began to rifle through the outfits that would make the cut to be packed for the upcoming trip. "The designer was only in town *that* night and I'd already been paid five *large* figures for that shoot."

"Right…" Alythia took care not to mask any of the sarcasm she was aiming for. "A little business won't hurt anything," she reasoned.

Myrna's mouth fell open and for an instant Alythia thought the woman had gone into shock.

"Are you serious right now, Alythia? One of our group is about to take the vows." Myrna curved a hand between two perky D-cups and put in place her most sincere expression. "*Vows,* Aly. Do you get how *huge* this is?"

Oh, I get it, Alythia thought. She got it all too well. No one, from the local media to the woman's closest friends, had been more surprised when bad girl around town Orchid Benjamin had announced not only an engagement but also an actual wedding date with her on-again, off-again flame, Jayson Muns. Yes, it was *huge.*

Melancholy took root inside Alythia, souring her interest in the snow globe perched in her lap. "I'm gonna be there with bells on for her, Mur," she said, returning the bauble to the white marble night table near the bed. She caught the quick look her friend sliced at her through the mirror.

"I'll be sure to give Orchid all the attention she needs." Aly debated slipping back into the rose-blush canvas shoes that matched the drop-tail hem top she wore with denim capris. Myrna didn't appear impressed or trusting of the promise.

Still, the woman shrugged. "At least you'll be there in body if not entirely in spirit."

Thankful for the reprieve, Aly resituated her head on the pillows and studied her anxious friend with greater interest. There was a noticeable weariness to Myrna, given her usual and almost annoying state of cheerfulness. After more than a few seconds of observation, she pushed herself up to half sit among the litter of clothes and pillows.

"What is it?" Alythia's demand was present in her amethyst eyes. The orbs contrasted beautifully against the dewy caramel of her skin.

"Don't pay me no mind, girl." She gave an airy wave. "This bridey stuff is already taking its zany effect on my mood."

"I don't buy it." Alythia raised her hand when Myrna opened her mouth to argue. "I already saw the expression, so spill it."

"I'm just being stupid."

"Okay…" Alythia's drawling reply noted that she wasn't about to argue her friend's insight.

Myrna's smile was more genuine despite the slight strain she couldn't quite shadow. She tossed a blouse at Alythia's face.

"Aly?"

"Yeah?"

Myrna moved the clothes to be packed, clearing a spot to sit on the armchair. "What do you think about

Orchid's engagement?" she queried in a tiny voice, as though someone might overhear them even though they were completely alone in the monster penthouse apartment Myrna kept in downtown Charlotte.

"Why?" Again, Aly pushed herself up a smidge higher on the bed. When Myrna just watched her, she shrugged. "I mean, I'm happy…." She shook her head, certain that there was more to the question.

"I'm happy, too." Myrna scooted to the edge of the chair. "But don't you think it's all a little too-too soon?"

"*You're* asking this?" Alythia's words were half matter-of-fact and half playful.

Myrna Fisher was one of the most sought-after lingerie models in the country. The fact that she was black made the accomplishment even more noteworthy. Still, for all Myrna's savvy allure, her weakness was for relationships. It was well known that the lovely model didn't go long without a man on her arm. The woman so adored relationships that she had a tendency to become suffocating—a thing most men didn't handle well, regardless of the woman's beauty.

Moreover, it did Myrna's reputation no favors to end things with one adoring suitor only to have another one before the close of the following week.

Appearing somewhat offended by Alythia's response, Myrna pushed off the chair and returned to holding outfit possibilities before herself in the mirror. "Unlike our friend, at least *I* don't pick up random guys to take home."

Alythia kept her eyes downcast, allowing wavy jaw-length tresses to shield her expression from Myrna's sight. Myrna's usual defense was one of many. To her, partners were significant others. No one seemed to have the heart to tell Myrna those "others" were significant only in *her* mind.

"People can change, Mur."

"Sure they can, but do people change *that* much in the span of two weeks?"

"What do you know?" Alythia tilted her head in an attempt to spy Myrna's actual face rather than its reflection in the mirror.

Myrna was cagey, pretending to be involved in her outfits. "There's nothing that I can prove." She suddenly whirled around to point a finger in Alythia's direction. "And I'm *not* jealous."

Aly didn't think it was wise just then to challenge the vehement declaration as a lie in spite of what she saw lurking in Myrna's brown eyes.

Alythia Duffy and her close circle of acquaintances had been friends since middle school. They'd been through tense times but always stuck up for each other and defended each other whether or not that defense was warranted.

Though with age came a certain clarity, Alythia thought to herself. There were times when one had to see another for what he or she really was. By all accounts, Orchid Benjamin's reputation had been tarnished by one sexual disgrace after another since high school.

"I just don't know if getting married is the best idea for her, that's all," Myrna continued.

Alythia, who was now seated in the middle of the bed with her legs folded beneath her, tuned back into Myrna's diatribe. "Are you suggesting that we say something to change her mind about going through with the wedding?"

The question tugged Myrna's rapt attention off the mirror and the gossamer lounge dress she was debating over. Again she looked to Alythia and gave a smug gaze. "I'll reserve judgment till I get a bead on the happy couple during our fun-filled getaway."

Gage Vincent was well respected; his reputation was well earned from his fellow industrial entrepreneurs. That respect turned into merited admiration with a hint of envy when the discussion fixed on his stunning success with the opposite sex. It was regarded with an abundance of love when his close circle of friends was in the vicinity.

Gage had known his riotous crew since the days of their rough-and-tumble boyhoods. College and grad school had split the foursome for several years but the bonds hadn't been broken. The four often traded war stories over drinks, dinner, games of cards or games of a more athletic variety.

While not linked by business, Jayson Muns, Zeke Shepard and Dane Spears were quite appreciative of the fact that Gage's business saved them the expense of having to purchase their own modes of air travel.

Orchid Benjamin wasn't overly impressed. The private aircraft had bold silver streaks trekking both sides of the fuselage to meet at the fin to form the letters *VID*. Not that the plane wasn't dumbfoundingly impressive and then some, Orchid thought. What gnawed at her was that her fiancé hadn't had the good taste and judgment to purchase one of his own.

"I mean, what are we gonna do on future trips?" Orchid asked the woman who had exited the limo behind her. "I know he doesn't expect me to fly commercial." She shivered as though the idea were too awful to dwell upon.

"He probably didn't see the need, Ork." Myrna pulled sunglasses from her head and perched them across the bridge of her nose. "What for? When his best friend has three of them?"

The rationale apparently pacified Orchid enough. She ran across the tarmac to greet her intended with a throaty—and, in Myrna's opinion, theatrical—kiss.

Two men stood a few feet away from the affectionate couple. Myrna immediately cast them as friends of the groom. As the other men in her line of sight were in some variation of uniforms, it was a logical guess. From the way they stood back on long legs, hand over mouths, heads inclined toward each other, it also wasn't hard to guess the topic of their private chatter.

Myrna had been part of enough staged photo settings to have a fairly passable grasp on reading body language. Yep, she thought, Ork's rep had surely preceded her on the trip. The surge of an approaching engine caught her ear and Myrna let go of a bit more of her apprehension. She released a purely girlish shriek and hurried over to greet the fourth member of their circle.

"How'd you guys manage to swing leaving town without the entire local media descending?" Jeena Stewart placed a hand across her brow while observing the jet in the distance.

"They say Gage Vincent can swing anything." Myrna dropped a kiss on Jeena's cheek when they pulled out of their embrace. "Guess that includes leaving town without the whole world knowing about it."

Jeena nodded, sudden weariness drawing her face

into a tight honey-toned mask. "I wish returning my phone calls were one of those things that he could swing."

Myrna masked her smile, knowing Jeena would take it as an insult. Word was—and speculation ran high toward that *word* being fact—that Jeena Stewart owed her fortune to the world's oldest profession. There was nothing anyone could prove, however. Part of the reason for unsubstantiation lay in the fact that Jeena could claim clients for her so-called dating service at local and national government levels, or so it was rumored. Additionally, the woman ran her business like a...well...like a business, with salary and benefits for employees—female *and* male.

Myrna thought it was all absurd, hence her suppressed, knowing smile. "Guess we're about ready to take off." She noted the limo driver passing off her luggage to a member of the baggage staff. "Of course, we're still one short." She spared another glance across the tarmac.

Jeena rolled her eyes. "Why am I not surprised?"

"Ah...dammit," Alythia said in disgust.

She had hoped taking her car, as opposed to hiring a driver, might play into her excuse of bad traffic, which would have resulted in her missing out on the luxurious flight.

But to her dismay, she arrived at the airstrip to find the plane still waiting. A chorus of birds were chirping somewhere amid the late-morning air as if they meant to welcome her to fun and excitement. Alythia appreciated the welcome but all the while considered circling back to the interstate in hopes of getting caught up in a traffic jam—a tad unlikely at that time of day, but who knew? It all could work in her favor and she might get—

"Can I help you with those?"

Alythia turned, her jaw dropping while her eyes zoned out in a show of surprise.

"Lucky." She breathed the completion of her thought aloud.

She wasn't sure if the man who stood within touching distance had sparked such a reaction because of his height. She stood just shy of five-ten in her bare feet, but this guy had to be six-two at least. Sure, it could've been the height or the muscular build—more lean than massive. Alythia was more inclined to wager on the man's remaining attributes.

Whoever he was, he had the most remarkable shade of skin, an unblemished tone of black coffee. The richness was offset by a long, steady brown gaze enhanced by overt gold flecks. His hair was straight textured and close-cropped. Thanks to the morning's powerful sunrays, Alythia could tell that his hair was of the same deep brown as his eyes.

He was smiling and the curve of a beckoning sculpted mouth was made more attractive by the singular dimple accompanying it. Still, that stare of his was impossible to ignore and difficult to perceive as anything other than intensely observant. His gaze also lent a well-blended mixture of heat and cool to his smile.

"Are you okay?"

She heard him speaking to her, his smile carrying more heat when he leaned close to ask how she was. He extended a hand as if he meant to cup her elbow but barely let his thumb graze the bend of her arm.

Alythia ordered—no, begged—the sudden and completely uncharacteristic desire to moan to cease and desist with the pressure it applied to her larynx.

"I, um— I'm good," she managed, and then followed up the lie with a laugh. "I *was* good before I got here and saw that my ride was kind enough not to leave without me."

He roared into laughter, the sound causing Alythia to jump at the full honesty of it. Despite the contagious effect of the reaction, she winced when he looked her way.

"Sorry, I know I sound ungrateful," she said.

Curiosity intermingled with his amusement. "Why do you think you're ungrateful?"

"Most people dream of visiting the Caribbean." She looked toward the jet once more. "Of those who have actually had those dreams come true, few get there on a private plane."

"Um, could I take that stuff for you?" he inquired of her bags again before the dumbfounded amusement on his face started to make her feel uneasy.

"Sorry. Um…" Aly began to relinquish her bags. "Thanks for your help— Oh, wait."

Easing the strap of a tan duffel over his shoulder, he watched her fumble through a plump midsize purse.

"Dammit…I knew I had a five or ten in here…."

"Hey." He cupped her elbow that time. "There's no need to tip me."

Alythia blinked toward the plane. "I'm pretty sure you guys are way behind schedule because of me."

"We'll get there." He voiced the soft reassurance while applying a light massage to the elbow he cupped. "They aren't gonna leave without you." He winced a little against the sun in his eyes when he glanced at the plane. "This is a vacation. No clocks. Say it. 'No clocks.'"

"No clocks." Alythia nodded in a hypnotic manner while repeating the phrase that sounded like heaven. "No clocks." She gave in to a smile that demanded to be seen.

Clarity surged in the liquid chocolate of Gage Vincent's stare and he realized that the woman standing before him had no idea that the plane was his or who he was for that matter.

He dipped his head to peer into Alythia's eyes and observed her that way for several seconds. He nodded, evidently satisfied that her outlook was improving and more than a little captivated by the stunning shade of her gaze. He then took four of her five bags, effortlessly hoisting the straps across his shoulders and angling one at his neck.

Alythia held on to an overnight case—the smallest of the five. Her smile brightened in approval of the button-down shirt he wore. The short sleeves revealed the flex and ripple of well-toned muscle accentuated by the flawless café noir of his skin.

"Shall we?" He motioned her ahead with the hand secured about the handle of a boxy brown-and-beige case.

"Do you think your boss will be a jerk about me holding up the party?" Alythia asked once they were crossing the tarmac toward the waiting plane.

"You're good." He paused. "The man's a sucker for women. Especially women who look like you."

"Thank you." Her words were delivered coolly enough even though his remark had threatened to halt her stride. "Um…will you be on the flight or…?"

"You'll see me around." He halted at the foot of the mobile stairway.

"Thank you." Aly made no secret of the fact that she was attempting to memorize his face before she headed on up the steps leading into the plane.

Gage's smile went from friendly to smoldering within seconds of Alythia's exit. He thought her legs seemed to go on forever beneath the airy white skirt that flared above her knees. She wore an emerald racer-back tank that matched strappy sandals that added emphasis on trim ankles and shapely calves. Not until one of the actual baggage handlers interrupted his survey to ask for the cases did Gage look away.

Chapter 2

Gage inclined his head a fraction as though he were attempting to obtain a better view of what he was observing. Absently, he moved the back of one hand across the sleek whiskers that had just started to shadow the strong curve of his jawline. He'd probably have a full beard by the end of the trip, he mused, still staring fixedly at the screen of his MacBook Air.

The golden flecks lurking in the liquid brown of his gaze seemed to sparkle more vividly. He was putting forth a more diligent effort to view the small square footage of space in the same light as the man he video-conferenced with did.

"Sorry, Clive...it's just not working for me," he said, at last accepting defeat.

"That's because you're not seeing it through a tourist's eyes." Clive's voice rippled out through the laptop's speakers.

"I resent that." Gage put up an obviously phony show of being insulted. "I'm as much of a tourist as the next man."

"Woman," Clive corrected. "You also need to see this place through the eyes of a woman."

Clive's robust and genuine laughter rumbling then, Gage raised his hands defensively. He reclined in the swivel chair behind an efficient but more than adequate desk in the office aboard the aircraft.

"You've finally lost me…completely. I'm afraid this requires an expertise that I'm not in any way sorry to say I don't have."

"Are you for real?" Clive was incredulous when the screen split and he appeared on the monitor. Soon, though, he relented with a decisive shake of his head. "Look, G, I don't need you to actually *see* my plans here." He referred to the space along the quaint side street within the resort he owned. "I only need you to tell me that you believe the venture has moneymaking potential."

Gage replayed the clip that had provided a 360-degree tour of the space in question. The area was practically shielded from view due to the overgrown foliage. The camera turned away from the space to offer a brief presentation of the cobblestone street that boasted a twenty-four-hour breakfast bar, nail, wax and massage spa, as well as a bookshop, among its other sole proprietorships.

"Definitely has diversity going for it," Gage murmured, while more avidly assessing the locale.

Via split screen, Clive could be seen rubbing his hands palm to palm. He even seemed to be performing a little excited dance in his chair, the back of which could be seen moving to and fro through the screen.

"Well?" Clive's baby-blue eyes were wide with expectancy.

Smirking with evident devilry driving the gesture, Gage let his old friend sweat out the wait for a few more seconds. "I want to take a look at the site when we land, but based on what's before me now...I can see it."

Clive bowed his head and Gage's smirk turned into a grin when he heard the man's delighted grunt drift through the laptop's speaker. While Gage hadn't truly been able to visualize Clive's business plan for the space at his resort property, Gage saw money. And when Gage Vincent saw money, money was made.

A chuckle accompanied Gage's grin as Clive's excitement infected him to an extent. "When'd you get so interested in fashion?"

"Well, hell, Gage, we can't all be *GQ* superstars, now, can we?" From the screen, Clive waved a hand toward Gage, who looked worthy of a spread in the famed magazine even in the simple button-down shirt, its cream color accentuating the flawless pitch of his skin.

"I still know what I like, though," Clive finished indignantly.

Gage's chuckling rounded out on a quick laugh. He traded stroking his jaw for massaging it and more closely regarded his friend. "Is it the fashion you like or the woman who gave you this idea?"

It was Clive's turn to raise his hands in defense. "I swear it's the money the fashion can make me." The quirky smile that always betrayed his attempts to be at his most serious betrayed Clive then. "The woman only helped me to see it through her eyes."

Gage's infectious, hearty laughter erupted. "Is she a blonde or brunette?" he queried through his laughter.

Clive buffed his nails against the crimson polo shirt he wore. "Neither," he replied.

"Mmm...redhead, then." Gage was confident with his guess until Clive sent him a look of mock smugness through the screen.

"Not..." Gage observed the easy arrogance in Clive's resulting smile and fell into another roll of laughter. "Try and save a few of the sistas for the rest of us, will you?" he asked when he'd come up for air. The teasing pleas held a fair amount of seriousness. Gage knew that his old college roommate fully earned his ladies'-man status.

"You and your counterparts are safe." Clive leaned back in his desk chair. Behind him a view of swaying palms and unending turquoise water rippled in the distance. "Besides, this lady is only interested in me for my building."

"Good for her. Smart in business and too smart to fall for your foolish lines."

"Hey! My lines are gold." Clive shook his head in spite of himself and appeared a touch serious. "You're right, though—she's a smart one. Ambitious, too. *That* combined with your assurance that there is more money in my future is enough for the time being. Besides—" the playful light returned to Clive's expression "—it's going to take a lot of time to get the place in shape. That's more than enough time for me to put my wooing skills to work."

Smiling broadly, Gage shook his head, as well.

"Be sure to let me know how that works out for you." He wiped at a laugh tear in the corner of his eye and straightened in his chair when he took notice of his open doorway.

The woman from the tarmac waved a hand but began to back out of the office. Gage motioned her forward. Satisfied that she was obliging his request, he interrupted Clive midsentence.

"C? Listen I need to go, but we'll catch up as soon as we land, all right?"

"Sounds good. See you then." Clive signed off with a mock salute just before his side of the split screen went black.

"I'm sorry, I didn't realize you were on a call." She bit the side of her lip, watching as he closed down the laptop.

"Come on in." Gage was done with the computer and rounded the desk while giving her another beckoning wave.

She hadn't taken more than a few steps into the office. There she remained. "I only came to apologize."

"Apologize?" His playful frown prefaced a smile. "Now you *have* to come in."

His hand folded down over her elbow, drawing her into the small, albeit state-of-the-art, work space. Despite her reluctance to move forward, she let herself be led into the smartly done office.

"Wow…" She blinked several times in rapid succession, turning to assess every element of the room.

Gage allowed himself to marvel, as well. Sure, he'd marveled over her looks—what man wouldn't? She was tall and possessed more than her fair share of soft curves, as well as a fragile allure that belied a certain strength. The radiant, creamy caramel of her skin, the stunning amethyst tinge of her stare and the wavy tousle of blue-black bobbing about that lovely face had captured a great deal of his interest. Still, her heart-stopping physical assets didn't explain the extent of his attention.

What was it exactly? It annoyed him that he couldn't put a finger on it and yet it beckoned him just the same. Gage believed that once he managed to pinpoint the "it," he wouldn't be nearly as infatuated with her as he surely felt he was becoming.

"Alythia Duffy."

He realized she was giving her name and offering her hand once he'd eased out of the deep well of his thoughts. Taking the hand she extended, he didn't shake it, only squeezed and held. His grip hinted of possession and gave no promise of freedom.

Alythia cleared her throat.

"You weren't out there when the introductions went around earlier and I—" She cast a quick look toward the doorway. "I, um… I missed the first 'getting to know you' session because I was running sort of late."

"Right…" Gage allowed unfairly long lashes to settle over his warm gaze as though he were just recalling that fact. "Right…*happily* late till you discovered your ride *hadn't* left without you."

Alythia hung her head when her eyes closed. Gage could feel her hand going limp inside his and he gave it a few reassuring pumps in an attempt to pull her gaze back to his. It worked.

"Gage Vincent."

"I know." Alythia then placed her free hand over the one he'd clasped about hers.

She'd bowed her head again and moved a smidge closer and he took the opportunity to inhale deeply of the light fragrance she wore.

"I'm so sorry about before." Alythia raised her head suddenly.

"You've already apologized to me twice at least and we haven't even known each other a full day."

"Oh, I'm—" Alythia appeared to be piping up to extend more apologies. Again she bowed her head. "I didn't mean to mistake you for working here."

"Why?" Gage faked confusion, although he knew very well what had her so distressed. "I employ a great group of folks." He shrugged. "It's nice to be thought of as one of them."

"But I shouldn't have assumed—"

"Why not? I offered to take your bags, didn't I?"

"Yes, but—"

"You weren't rude to me, were you?"

"I—" Alythia paused. "I guess not," she said finally.

Imprisoning her hand in both of his then, Gage squeezed again, using the gesture to tug her closer. "You weren't. Trust me, I know what rude is." Briefly, his liquid stare shifted left as though he were about to look across his shoulder.

Alythia piped up once more, this time in order to champion her friends. "The trip hit us out of nowhere. I'm afraid we're all sort of…um…discombobulated." She pressed her lips together.

Gage's eyes locked on her plump bronze-glossed mouth. Silently, he commanded his focus to reside on her words, for the time being, at least.

"Orchid's your typical nervous bride. I guess we're

all nervous." Alythia sounded as though she was speaking the last bit to herself.

Gage narrowed his gaze, cocking his head inquisitively in hopes that she'd elaborate on the last. Instead, she fixed him with a dazzling smile that he admitted pleased him just as much as any clarification she might have given.

"I just don't want us to get off on the wrong foot. It's important for Orchid that the trip goes well and I can't afford to be the one that shoots it all to hell."

Gage felt the wicked flex of muscle along his jaw. "And why should all of that rest on you?"

Alythia responded with a laugh that was clearly tension filled. "There are many 'whys,' Mr. Vincent. Among them my inability to be on time when there's fun to be had." She rolled her eyes. "I don't mean to ramble. Like I said, we're all a little nervous."

Nodding, Gage used the hand he still held captive to pull her arm through the crook of his. "Well, the least an aircraft employee can do is to find a way to settle a passenger's nerves."

With that, he escorted Alythia from the office.

Two delicious mojitos later, Aly was feeling less nervous and far more amused. The dynamics emerging among the newly collected group kept a genuine smile on her face. Whether it was the group or the mojitos that deserved such credit, she couldn't wager a guess.

Gage had escorted her out to the main cabin and had gotten her settled into a seat somewhat removed from where the rest of the group had gathered. He'd then personally seen to filling the order for her drink.

Alythia kept her gaze trained outside the windows

on purpose. She knew Gage's innocent act of kindness was already being rehashed by her friends.

"How are those nerves doin'?"

Smiling at the question, Alythia looked up at Gage while raising her third mojito, which she was only half-way through. "The nerves are much better."

Gage claimed a spot on one of the milk-chocolate suede swivels across from where Alythia relaxed. "And how's the view?"

"The view can't at all be complained about."

"Hmph."

The response drew her stare and she studied him with a knowing intensity. "Guess this is all pretty old hat to you, huh?"

"How often do you travel, Alythia?" he asked, angling an index finger alongside his temple while he watched her.

She turned her attention back outside the window. "Quite a bit, but first class has nothing on this."

"Well, it doesn't get old for me," Gage shared, swiveling his chair a bit. "Every time I take a flight, take time to pull my face out of a report and take a look at the view, I'm reminded of how blessed I am."

"Must've been a hard road to get here."

Gage grinned. "*Hard* would've been nice. My road was about ten times beyond hard."

"Ha! I can relate!" Alythia laughed.

"How so?"

Alythia wasn't of a mind to elaborate. "We're talking about *your* hard road, not mine."

"I'd trade my hard-luck story for yours any day."

"I'd hate to sour your mood for the rest of the trip, and *my* story would surely do that." She sipped at a bit more of the mojito, loving the rejuvenating effects of the crisp drink.

"What if I told you my story could have the same effect on you?"

"All right, then." Alythia faced him fully, her elbows propped along the arms of the chair. "Suffice it to say that my hard-luck story makes me very appreciative of every good thing that comes my way." For effect she raised her mojito in a mock toast.

There was a burst of feminine laughter, followed by the roar of male chortling and additional feminine giggling. The sounds drew quick smiles from both Gage and Alythia.

"Sounds like your friends share your point of view."

Bewilderment sent the elegant lines of Alythia's brows closer, though she didn't remain stumped for long. "We've all weathered storms and learned from them."

"Is that right?" He pretended to be stunned.

Alythia rolled her eyes playfully. "Even rich girls have storms to weather, Mr. Vincent." She aimed a soft smile in Orchid's direction.

"Hey, Gage?" Myrna called from across the cabin. "Are we gonna fly above the clouds for the whole flight? I want to see the water."

"Appreciative of every good thing, huh?" Gage spoke the words for Alythia's ears only and then pushed out of his chair. "Finish your drink." He squeezed her shoulder on his way to join the group.

"So?"

"Gage was popping the cap on his Samuel Adams when Dane Spears's question reached his ear.

"So." Gage took a swig of the beer.

"Don't even try it." Dane's soft admonishment accompanied a playful frown. "What's the story?" he persisted.

"What story?" Gage leaned against the Blackwood counter space inside the bar area where his friend had cornered him.

"Come off it, G. You obviously already picked yours."

Gage eased a measuring look toward his beer bottle. "I think I already had too much to drink." He shook his head at Dane. "What the hell are you talkin' about?"

"Don't take offense, G. Hell, she's—she's beautiful." Dane voiced the compliment as though he was in disbelief of an absolute truth. "If she hadn't been so late to the party, I'd have probably already staked my claim."

Grinning as realization hit home, Gage gave another shake of his head. "This isn't a date." He downed another swig of the tasty brew.

"Who said anything about a date? I'm talkin' about a sure thing." Dane helped himself to one of the assortment of beers chilling in a tub of ice next to the bar. He used the bottle he'd selected to motion toward the women across the room.

"Fine as hell and sure things, every one of 'em."

Gage narrowed a look toward his friend. "Every one?"

"Well…except the bride, of course."

"Of course." Gage enjoyed a few more swallows of beer and enjoyed the view across the room. The view of Alythia Duffy was one that he especially enjoyed. Whether or not he realized it, or would have admitted it if he had.

"Have you met them before?"

Dane settled back against the bar. His arms folded across the snug workout top meant to emphasize an already broad chest as he affixed a keener interest upon the group. "Haven't formally *met* any of them, but anybody who's watched TV or read a paper knows 'em in one form or another. Except for your girl," he said, referencing Alythia. "Keeps to herself. She's a beauty but seems kinda standoffish now that I've met her."

Gage smiled, recognizing the last remark as Dane-speak for "She turned me down." He enjoyed another gulp of the beer, silently admitting that he was as glad of that fact as he was of the appearance of Dane's sulking.

Alythia being relatively unknown pleased him greatly. What pleased him even more was the fact that she didn't claim the kind of status her friends seemed to relish.

"Quiet ones are usually the biggest freaks," Dane chimed in as if reading Gage's thoughts. He shrugged. "I'm just saying that it doesn't look like we'll have to put much work into getting a little somethin' somethin' above- or belowground, is all."

Gage poised his bottle for another swig and changed his mind. "Don't believe everything you read," he cautioned.

"Oh, trust me, my friend. Everything I know about that trio, I didn't have to read."

Instead of drinking from the bottle, Gage pressed it to his forehead, needing the cool to breach his skin. "Don't do this," he sighed. "It's not the time for conspiracies."

"That much I know." Dane seemed to sober. "Already gave it my best shot and Jay's still over the moon for this one."

Gage finally pinned his friend with an expression that harbored no trace of amusement. "What'd you do?"

"Felt Jay had a right to know the word on the street about her." Dane shrugged, downed a bit of the Budweiser he'd selected. "That fool tends to dwell in his own world, you know?"

"Yeah, minding his own business, finding a woman he wants to spend the rest of his life with… Lotta men would love living in that world."

"Don't even try it, G." Dane used his bottle to point in Gage's direction. "Hookin' up with the wrong chick can turn a beautiful life into hell on earth."

"Where's all this comin' from, man?"

"Coming from one friend to another."

"Jay might not see it that way." Gage went back to girl watching and nursing his beer.

"We usually don't see it *that way* when being told something for our own good."

"Right." Gage left Dane's counter-remark unchallenged and pushed away from the bar. "Guys, we can take this stairway down to find our lunch!" he called out to the rest of the group.

Gage waited for Alythia, offering her his arm when she broke away from her friends.

"Thanks." She leaned into him a little. "Those mojitos were no joke."

"There's more where they came from."

Alythia tilted back her head. "That's good to know. Being around my girls for ten days will definitely put me in the mood for more."

Gage slanted a look toward Dane, who responded with a mock toast of his beer bottle. "I know what you mean," he said.

Chapter 3

It went without saying that the lower deck of the jet made quite an impression on Gage Vincent's guests. Myrna and Orchid were very vocal in their appreciation of the sumptuous layout of the combination dining room and sitting room. Myrna oohed and aahed while breaking into a light sprint down the wide aisle. She trailed her fingers across the silk-covered beige sofas and chairs with embroidered finishes. Even Orchid, who had seen her fair share of private jets, seemed impressed by the understated decor of the grand space. She didn't let too much of it show, preferring instead to use the opportunity to school her fiancé. Simply put, if Jayson was confused about what to look for when he bought his jet, use *this* for an example.

Jeena was equally as impressed. She was busy trying to get Gage to agree to a time when they might chat.

"I know neither of us are in the mood to discuss business, but you're so busy every time I call," Jeena rambled while tapping furiously at her mobile as she scrolled through the calendar there. "I'm pretty sure your assistant is sick and tired of talking to me while we try to work on a good time to meet. But I'm flexible with whatever we can…"

While Jeena talked, Gage only half listened. It was of no consequence. If need be, he could have recited her spiel verbatim. A good thing, too, because taking a more avid interest in the woman's rambling wasn't a top priority just then.

Gage kept his gait to a leisurely stroll.

So much the better for Jeena. She hoped she might be on the verge of nailing down a meeting with the elusive entrepreneur. Aside from her, the one thing Jeena's… clients all had in common was Gage Vincent. They were either *in* business with the man or they wanted to be. Jeena hoped to be on the *in* business with Gage Vincent side of things. Having him on her side to smooth the way regarding certain ventures would be a coup indeed. But Jeena didn't realize that she was pretty much carrying the conversation alone, with only Gage's intermittent "mmm-hmms" to punctuate the discussion.

"I'll have my assistant get in touch with you," he managed just as they rounded the corner into the dining area. He didn't spare Jeena a glance. His stirring gaze was set on Alythia as he and Jeena walked into the room, among the last to arrive.

Gage saw the smile enhancing Alythia's profile when she angled her head to look up at the recessed lighting that added a golden glow to the cream, beige and cocoa color scheme. The space was devoid of windows, and woodgrain-based lamps had been added to provide warm illumination. Gage dipped his head, hoping to shield the smile that emerged as he studied her reaction.

"And here I thought the bottom of a plane was only for storing luggage," Aly teased. Turning just as Gage looked up, she favored him with a smile across her shoulder.

Alythia's comment closed off whatever attention Gage had been paying to Jeena.

"So when should I expect your assistant's...call?" Jeena finished disapprovingly when she saw Gage walk on ahead to catch up with her friend.

Jeena's cool, unreadable smile mimicked the one Zeke Shepard wore when he rounded out the group arriving in the dining space. He'd taken a deep interest in the sight of his old friend leaving one beauty to catch up with another.

"My friend has a one-track mind sometimes," Zeke noted to the petite woman Gage had left behind.

Jeena ceased working at her phone. "One-track?" she queried of the slender dark man next to her.

"One reason Gage agreed to this trip is because all of Orchid's friends are dimes." Zeke grinned.

"That's cold," Jeena chided, though lightly. She pulled a stylus pen from her bag and blandly regarded the man in question. "I'd like to think he really wanted to do something special for his friend."

"Well...that, too." Zeke gave a little shrug. "But being surrounded by four beautiful women won't be a hardship."

"Hmph." Jeena tapped a finger to her cheek and slowed her pace a bit. "Are you saying that he plans to sleep with all of us?"

"Nah." Zeke's response was softer, reassuring then. "My man's already made his selection."

Jeena stroked the soft hair tapered into a V at her nape while studying Gage and Alythia. The two stood discussing an oil canvas that was on display inside a cozy alcove a ways down from the dining room. She gave a sideways glance up at Zeke.

"And what about you? Have you made your selection, as well?"

"Not much point in making a selection if your choice is otherwise occupied, is there?" He gave a pointed look toward Jeena's phone.

"Oh, this?" Shrugging, Jeena dipped into a sultrier mode. "It'll do until something better comes along." She used one hand to tuck the phone into the back pocket of her coral linen capris; the other she linked through the crook of Zeke's arm.

"You live very well," Alythia told Gage once he had finished the story of how he'd acquired the piece adorning the alcove wall.

"Thanks." He gave her a gracious nod. "It's not without a lot of hard work."

"Just don't work too hard," Alythia advised with a playful gleam in her light eyes.

"Don't work too hard without having anything interesting to show for it." Gage edited the advice and then smiled encouragingly. "Would you agree?"

Aly regarded the vibrant hues that seemed to shimmer within the canvas and draw the observer's eye to the brilliant meshing of colors. "I'd definitely agree." She sighed as though imagining herself in the seascape depicted in the painting. "I might get around to living that truth if I ever get past the 'working hard' phase."

Gage turned his attention back toward the canvas. "This trip's a good place to start."

"It was supposed to be." Alythia couldn't resist sending an uncertain glance across her shoulder.

"What's that look for?"

It wasn't in her nature to confide so easily, but the man possessed the most coaxing voice. Aly wondered if he knew that and how often the attribute worked to his advantage. Her guess was *quite* often.

"The only reason I agreed to come along on this getaway was because there's a chance for me to get some real business handled."

"Real business, huh? In the Caribbean?" Gage's rich, dark brows rose.

The soothing depths of the man's voice notwithstanding, Alythia had been bursting to share her news. Silently, she reasoned that she could at least count on Gage not to blab to her girls if she told him.

"I happened upon a business opportunity while I was trying to find a little more info on where we were heading for this trip. I hope to own a chain of boutiques one day." She shrugged. "Right now there's only two, but I'm looking to expand. Turns out our resort owner has a shopping village that he's hoping to cultivate. I've convinced him to at least consider giving my shop a chance."

Gage put in a fantastic effort to school his expression.

"We should go check out the place when we land, all right?"

Alythia was already shaking her head no to Gage's suggestion. "It's not necessary and I don't want to men-

tion it to my friends. They're still getting over the shock
that I agreed to come along." She folded her arms across
the emerald tank that hugged her breasts adoringly.

"It'd crush Ork to know that my priority is once
again business and not taking time out with my girls."

Gage's grimace over the outlook triggered the lone
dimple in his cheek. "Time out with friends takes
money."

"Agreed," she said with a smirk, "but my friends
think the way I earn my money takes up too much
time." She cast a withering look toward the painting
then. "Unfortunately, I don't come from money—" she
looked to Orchid "—I'm not model material—" she took
note of Myrna "—and I don't have the nerve to earn my
money the way *they say* Jeena earns hers."

"That's good to hear." He leaned in close and gave
her waist a pat. "And you're wrong. You're definitely
model material and then some."

Alythia felt her lips part, but she really didn't expect to handle the task of filling her mouth with words.
Thankfully, speaking became a moot point when Gage
turned once again, offering her his arm and then escorting her toward the dining room area, where everyone
else had already gathered.

Dining room seating consisted of blocky chairs with
heavily cushioned seats and backs. A booth seat ran the
length of a polished dark oak table and was upholstered
in the same embroidered beige silk as the dining chairs
and other furnishings.

The space could seat six comfortably, which mat-
tered little to the betrothed couple. They opted to enjoy
the late lunch on the sofa that held position opposite
the dining table and ran the length of the entire space.

There, Orchid and Jayson lounged in a loving tangle of arms and legs. Every now and then, Orchid would burst into wild laughter over something that her fiancé whispered in her ear.

Across from the happy couple, other companion selections appeared to have been made. Dane and Myrna had laid claim to the booth seat while Zeke and Jeena engaged in their own private conversation from the cushiony chairs that put them side by side. Across from them, holding court at the other end of the table, were Alythia and Gage.

"Do you think our travel companions care what's on the menu?" Gage asked, reclining in the chair he occupied, elbow relaxed along the arm with his hand at his mouth as he spoke.

The question gave Alythia the chance to observe her friends, something she'd been trying *not* to do since the game of "choose your lunch partner" had gotten under way several minutes prior.

"I don't think it matters," she managed. Inwardly, Alythia was cringing. Jayson and Orchid's…demonstrativeness was understandable. The rest was, in Alythia's opinion, not a good idea. Not that she was in any way against enjoying all the delights a Caribbean getaway was supposed to offer. Only…if someone got the wrong idea and became disappointed, things would not bode well for the feelings of good cheer desired between the bride's and the groom's friends. From the looks of things, Aly noted, it didn't appear that anyone would be disappointed anytime soon.

From her periphery she could see Gage looking her way. She felt no pressure to make conversation. He was only…looking. She realized that he had a way of doing so that soothed instead of stirred her. Not that his gold-flecked browns didn't have the power to stir. There was just something about him, some element to his demeanor, that was intensely calming. It was a good thing, too, Aly thought. She was sure to require every calming agent she could summon before the end of the trip. She decided to give that train of thought as little brain time as possible and turned to face Gage fully.

"Forget them," she said. "*I'm* very interested in what's on the menu."

Chuckling softly, Gage pulled away the fist that supported his cheek. "I think you'd rather see it for yourself instead of listening to me trying to describe it."

Everyone, in fact, tuned in to the wait staff, who had arrived balancing trays of covered dishes and baskets of golden bread.

The late lunch was sort of a preamble to the kinds of delicacies the group was sure to enjoy during their ten-day Caribbean stay. The travelers dined on catfish, flown in fresh from the Outer Banks of North Carolina that morning, in a succulent white-wine-and-scallion sauce; chilled shrimp with a tangy tomato, orange and lemon glaze drizzle; steamed squash; and zucchini. There was fresh apple butter for the yeast bread and a decadent apple-cinnamon cobbler for dessert.

Once again private conversations and laughter resumed. The soft talking mingled with the infrequent clinking of silver- and other dinnerware.

"Tell me about your business." Gage took advantage of their measure of privacy to ease some of his curiosity about the woman dining to his right.

Alythia gave a one-shoulder shrug, keeping her light eyes downcast toward the zesty fish. "It's just a store."

His smile was equal parts desire and disappointment. "Why do you do that?" He clenched a fist to resist trailing his fingers along the caramel-toned length of her bare arm.

Again she shrugged. "I'm guessing that selling clothes would sound pretty silly compared to what you do all day." Faintly, she acknowledged that she really had no idea *what* he did all day.

"I don't think selling clothes is silly." Gage allowed mock bewilderment to cross his dark, attractive face. "I can think of at least three people in this room who I have *no* desire to see without their clothes."

Alythia tried to quiet her laughter when Gage fixed pointed looks upon each of his three best friends.

"Does your laughing mean you're in the mood to tell me how you got into the clothing business?" he asked.

Alythia took a moment to observe him then. He'd propped his fist to his cheek again and she wondered whether it was a habitual stance. Whatever the case, it kept her settled in a comfortable frame of mind conducive to talking.

Everyone appeared relaxed and truly involved in their conversations. The food—which was quickly disappearing—smelled wonderful and tasted even more wonderful. The room where they dined was as much like a work of art as the exquisite pieces that adorned the wall spaces of the aircraft.

Aly thought that the lamp lighting was soothing, very much like the sound of Gage's voice when he called her name to tug her from her thoughts.

"It's not such a surprise that I'd go into the clothing

business." She saw his probing stare narrow danger-
ously and raised her hands in a show of playful defense.
"I swear I'm not trying to make light of it."

Gage had dissolved into laughter. Once done, he relaxed back into the chair and waved his hand in a mock
show of permissiveness, urging her to continue with
her story.

At ease, Alythia forked up another plump glazed
shrimp. "I've always dreamed of being surrounded
by beautiful clothes." She popped the morsel of meat
into her mouth and took a moment to relish the taste.
"Mostly because I never had any growing up. None of
us did." Her expression saddened somewhat when she
looked toward Myrna and Jeena. "Then we met Orchid." She beamed.

"How'd *that* friendship happen?" Gage glanced
over to Orchid and Jayson. "I thought, with her family's money, she'd have been in some private school."

Aly levered a weighty look toward her friend. "Yeah,
she was, but there were…problems with following a
few choice rules and Mr. Benjamin said if she wanted
to rule-break, he wasn't gonna pay an arm and a leg for
her to do it. So he sent her to public school."

"Damn. I heard he was a tough man." Gage studied
Orchid for a moment or two and then shook his head.
"Hard to believe she got into so much trouble with a
parent like that."

"Well, Ork's always done her own thing…but Luther
Benjamin was a really great man." Alythia set down her
fork and leaned back into the chair, reminiscence filling her striking stare. "He never treated his daughter's
new public school girlfriends with anything other than

acceptance and respect. He was the kind of dad we all wanted." A sigh followed the admission.

"Wanted but…didn't have?" Gage carefully probed.

"Myrna's mom and dad separated when she was little." Alythia hugged herself a bit, raking her square French tips over suddenly chilled arms. "Jeena never knew her dad, and mine…" She resisted the urge to allow resentment to close her eyes. "Mine was in and out, in and out of my mother's pocketbook when he'd drank or gambled off his own. If he didn't steal it, she'd give it to him, no questions, no matter if she had to pay rent, buy food or…"

"Clothes."

His voice was quiet with understanding that made Aly smile while she nodded slowly.

"My mom died of a broken heart. She tried to be everything my father wanted. When that didn't work, she tried to buy his love and when that didn't work, she killed herself."

The stunning revelation was interrupted when a belt of laughter rang out from Zeke and Jeena's direction. Gage paid no mind to the outburst on the other side of the room. He appeared stricken and remorseful.

"Hell…" He groaned, having taken her elbow and drawn her so near to him that she was practically seated on the line between the cushions of his chair and her own. "God, I'm sorry for making you remember that."

"No, Gage." She smoothed her hand across the one that clutched her arm. "It wasn't like that. She—" Aly inhaled around the sudden emotion swelling her chest. "She passed slowly over time. There was nothing… physically wrong. She just didn't want to live—lost the will…"

"I'm sorry anyway." He squeezed her arm and gave it a little tug.

"Thanks." Her smile harbored none of its earlier somberness. "I'll never own up to the idea that I have any 'daddy issues.' My sister and I are too busy living our lives for that."

"I like the sound of that." Gage applied a soft thumb stroke to the bend of her arm.

"It's true. We live our lives in tribute to our mom." Suspiciously amused, he smiled. "How?"

The high back of the chair provided the perfect head-rest and Alythia indulged. "My sister is married to a pretty awesome guy who I'm not ashamed to say I'm just a little in love with."

Gage's whistle ushered in quick, hearty laughter. "Does your sister know this?"

"She does." Aly joined in when Gage laughed again. "Doesn't matter, though. The man only has eyes for her. He's been known to actually stop talking midsentence when she walks into a room. And that's just a *little piece* of what makes him so incredible." She sighed, but the sound held a dreamy vibe. "Men like him are in short supply."

Gage focused on where his thumb brushed Alythia's skin. "So while your sister is taking great men *off* the market, you're putting great clothes *on* it?"

Alythia's expressive gaze widened. "That's a fantastic way to look at it. Hmph, do you mind if I use that?"

Again he performed the permissive wave. "Not at all."

"Your attention, please."

The mixed conversations were interrupted then by

the sound of the captain's voice merging in among the warm drone of voices, clinking glasses and laughter.

"We are within thirty-five minutes of our arrival time and ask that you please begin your return to the main deck…"

"We'll have dessert and coffee upstairs, guys," Gage called out while the captain continued his message.

"Can we talk more later?" he asked Alythia while the others were pushing out of their seats.

Her smile brightened and she accepted when he offered her his hand.

"I'd like that," she told him, barely noticing the looks passing between the other couples at her and Gage's expense.

Chapter 4

As the captain's instructions hadn't demanded an *immediate* return to the main level, some decided to indulge in a few additional moments of getting acquainted. Alythia and Gage had the main cabin all to themselves for over fifteen minutes following the group's departure from the dining area. The bride and groom were the first to rejoin them.

Alythia didn't frown on Orchid's missing earring or too-tousled hair. A little lovemaking among the clouds would be the first of many happy memories for the soon-to-be-married couple, Alythia hoped.

Her contented thoughts about lovemaking at plus or minus forty thousand feet began to ebb when the last two "couples" arrived. Myrna was smoothing down flyaway tendrils of her straight shoulder-length bob. The gesture may not have seemed so out of place were it not for Dane. He strolled in behind Myrna and made no secret of drawing her back to him for a throaty kiss before he situated himself inside his jeans and tugged the zipper in place.

Zeke and Jeena proved to be a bit more discreet. They were not quite beyond the cabin's viewing range when Zeke plied Jeena's cheek with a parting kiss. He took it upon himself to secure the remaining few buttons on Jeena's blouse before they rounded the corner to join the others.

Alythia lost her taste for the drink she'd been watching Gage prepare. She reclaimed her spot along the window and far away from the main seating area. She'd been seated less than five minutes when a heavenly smell drifted beneath her nose. She found Gage setting two plates of the fragrant apple cobbler on the table between them. He retrieved their drinks from the bar and then took his place across from Alythia's seat and handed her one of the Baileys on the rocks.

When Aly looked his way, an understanding smile was tugging at the appealing curve of his mouth.

"It helps when you just ignore it," he said.

Aly didn't pretend to misunderstand. "And at what point does that become impossible?" she countered.

Gage sipped at his Baileys. "Been asking myself that for years," he muttered.

Aly raised her glass, set it down on the table and crumbled into uninhibited laughter. Gage joined her moments later.

Anegada, British Virgin Islands

Sitting farthest north of the British Virgin Islands was Anegada, a low, flat island known for its miles and miles of white-sand beaches and its commercial fishing success. While tourism served as the primary business on the island, the area was sparsely populated throughout much of the year. Alythia felt her well-being improve the moment she'd inhaled a few gulps of the floral air and absorbed the dazzling hues of blue and green that composed the environment.

Curiosity instigated a frown when she focused in on the local who had greeted them and was then shaking hands with Gage and his friends. By the time the man had made his way around to *her* friends, Aly knew exactly who he was.

"Clive Weeks?" she said before Gage could make the introductions. "Alythia Duffy," she supplied, watching the man's expression go from welcoming to surprised to stunned to pleased.

"Incredible!" he greeted, taking both of her hands in his and shaking them energetically.

"How?" Alythia looked to Gage, her meaning clear.

"College roommates," Gage and Clive explained in unison.

Alythia nodded but she didn't feel quite as at ease as she would've liked to at the moment.

"Absolutely incredible." Clive was pleased enough for them both.

The fact settled Alythia's suspicions somewhat. She was, however, very aware of her friends, whom she wasn't quite ready to share her business plans with. Thankfully, all the new lovers were still wholly absorbed with one another.

"C, why don't you let the woman get some rest before you load her down with business?" Gage suggested as though he'd sensed Alythia's reluctance to get too chatty with Clive around her friends.

"Right, right." Clive's baby blues registered apology and he gave Alythia's hands a final shake. "What was I thinking?"

"It's fine." Aly's smile was genuine. Clive's enthusiasm was very contagious.

"We'll talk tomorrow. Tonight is for fun." Clive left Alythia with a decisive nod before he turned to regain everyone else's attention. "Folks, the shuttle will be ready to carry us back to the resort in just a second!"

Jeena and Myrna had been conducting a silent inventory of the pier. For the time being, their minds seemed to be off the new men in their lives and on their surroundings.

"Clive? Will it be like this the entire time?"

Clive's accommodating smile never wavered. "What do you mean?" he asked Myrna.

"She means dead," Orchid said.

Alythia closed her eyes out of equal parts dread and mortification.

"You're about to be amazed," Clive promised, apparently taking no offense to the insult to his home.

From a brief conversation amid the group, Alythia learned that one year Clive had visited Anegada during the off-season. He'd taken an extended vacation from his once-thriving law practice in Greensboro, North Carolina, but he'd never gone back. He'd been in love with Anegada for ten years and mentioned that the love affair showed no signs of growing old.

"You guys are arriving, luckily, on the tail end of the storm season. It's also after our tourist season, as well," Clive continued. "That accounts for the lack of bodies,

but I can assure you that my resort, which is just outside Keel Point, is definitely not *dead*."

This news drew hearty laughter from everyone—
including Alythia, who had mixed a healthy dose of
relief into hers.

Clive stepped aside to speak with his shuttle driver.
In minutes he announced they were ready to set out.
Alythia celebrated the fact that Gage and his friends
were speaking with Clive and missing the conversation
while she and her girls boarded the shuttle. Just then,
Jeena was agreeing with Orchid that they would've expected for Gage to have a car waiting for them.

Anegada Weeks Resort was a play on Clive's sur-
name and a tribute to the love he had for the place he
called home. The multilevel main villa was a grand
structure that provided a spectacular view of any area
of the property.

Wide floor-to-ceiling windows were accentuated by
billowing drapes, filling the expansive, comfortably elegant rooms with refreshing breezes that mingled with
the scents from vast floral arrangements that decorated
every room, corridor and window.

Aside from the staff and grounds, only the guests
rivaled the resort for beauty. As Clive had promised,
the place was certainly not dead. While there wasn't an
overflow of bodies, the surroundings were more than
alive with the sounds of music, life and laughter. The
Weeks Resort boasted live music twenty-four hours a
day, seven days a week. The grooves were piped in to
all areas of the vibrant establishment, with the exception of the suites.

The amount and variation of the excitement must

have appeased Orchid, Jeena and Myrna, for they were quick to abandon their male love interests. Their plan was to follow the baggage carriers to their suites for a quick change of attire and then return to the array of bars, hot-tub lounges and poolside cafés for an afternoon of socializing.

As pleased by her friends' contentment as a mom leaving her squealing child with a sitter, Alythia envisioned an afternoon of sleep. She hoped her friends would find much to do and not miss her company for at least a couple of hours.

Aly could have kissed Clive Weeks when she discovered she and her girls had been spread out in suites along different wings of the resort. Satisfaction settled like a warm blanket the moment the door closed behind the polite porter. The middle-aged Haitian man must have sensed Alythia's exhaustion, for he bid her pleasant dreams before making his departure. Happiness manifested then in the form of a sigh when Aly marveled at the king bed with its four tall posters. The engraved mahogany supported gauzy curtains that puffed out in an elegant display thanks to the tropical breezes that circulated through the open windows. The broad frames were bumped infrequently by the heavy leaves of gigantic palm trees that danced wildly amid the wind.

Alythia approached the windows, wishing to be showered by the strong gusts of air. She discovered that there were fine screens behind the panes that admitted the sensational breeze and not much else.

The lullaby performed by the palm-tree leaves gradually returned Aly's thoughts to her desire for sleep. She'd kicked off her sandals and managed to exchange her travel clothes for a new pink-and-black sleep ensemble when the sound of jolly chimes mingled with the palm tree's song. Her mobile. She'd almost forgotten having taken it off airplane mode after they left the jet. Myrna and Jeena had suffered no bouts of amnesia. They'd made quick work of reminding everyone to rejoin the land of the living when they dug out their phones.

Tired as she was, Aly didn't resent answering the call when she saw the name on the faceplate.

"Well, hello!" she greeted her business manager.

"You sound awfully chipper." Marianne Young's husky voice would've sounded much deeper were it not for the underlying amusement that often colored her words.

"So how goes it?" Mari queried. "Any new scandals brewing?"

"Mari, shame on you," Alythia halfheartedly scolded while she placed her sandals in the elm-wood wardrobe across the bedroom. "Why would you think such a thing?"

"Oh, Lord…is it that bad?"

"Not yet. Suffice it to say that bed partners have already been selected and…tested."

Marianne whistled. "Wait a minute. How are you talking about this? Where is everyone else?"

"Separate suites, on separate wings of a huge resort."

Another whistle sang through the phone line. "Did you arrange that?" Marianne asked.

"Hmph." Aly wiggled her freed toes. "Not me. The fates did." She smiled when Marianne laughed.

"So? Any word?" she asked once the woman's chuckles softened.

"No decision has been made yet." Marianne needed

no clarity on what her client was referring to. Alythia had been in an almost-constant state of anxiety over the past few months. "Our proposal is sound, Aly. Try not to worry over this while you're there."

"Do you think there's anything more we can do to better our chances?" Aly persisted, perching on the arm of a deep chair near the open windows. "Maybe we could amp up our radio and TV advertisements. Do you think that might help?"

Marianne's laughter had returned. "Girl, you're too keyed up. You know that, right?"

"I know...." Alythia went boneless as she eased down into the chair, her long legs dangling over the arm. "I've been really edgy with the girls, too, and they don't deserve it. They're here to have fun, like I should be doing."

"Exactly." Marianne's strong voice was successful at driving home her encouragement. "We've done everything we can for the time being. Trust me, I've checked to see if we've left any stones unturned and I'll continue to check, all right?"

"All right."

"All we can do is wait."

"All we can do is wait." Alythia came down from her anxious high while repeating Marianne's precaution.

"Good. Now, you enjoy what I'm sure is gonna be an exquisite getaway."

"It *is* that." Aly closed her eyes as a strong breeze hit her face. "It's definitely that, but all I want to do right now is go to sleep."

"Well, there you go! I'm hanging up now. Sweet dreams..." Marianne's connection ended a second later.

"Sweet dreams indeed." Alythia sent a dreamy look in the bed's direction. She left the chair with the intention of placing her mobile on the stately elm-wood-and-bamboo nightstand. Rethinking that decision, she returned it to her overnight case. There was enough business to keep her occupied in Anegada without calling home for more.

Aly was on her way to bed when there was a knock. She stopped just short of the door to offer up a fast prayer that it be none of her friends. Not yet—she really needed just a couple of hours of downtime. Heck, she'd settle for *one* hour at this point.

Fortified by the prayer, she pulled open the door and let Gage witness her relief when she saw him in the hallway.

As relieved as Alythia was, though, Gage appeared anything but. A mixture of uncertainty had illuminated his dark, handsome face. "Is this a bad time?" He put obvious effort into asking the question.

"Going to bed." Aly rested her head on the side of the door. Her tone was lazy, eyelids heavy in anticipation of sleep.

"That part's obvious." A peculiar smile curved his fascinating mouth.

Alythia hadn't noticed him blatantly raking his beckoning stare along her body before. When he lowered his gaze in a more direct manner that time, she took heed and received her second round of mortification for the day.

She'd been so focused on praying for it not to be her BFFs on the other side of the door that she had completely dismissed what she was wearing when she opened it.

Gage briefly set his hand across his mouth to shield a broadening smile as she bolted from the door to go in search of a robe.

He shut the room door and followed her deeper into the suite. In the bedroom he leaned back against the door and indulged in the long, unconscious glimpses she offered of surprisingly shapely limbs and other plump assets that were emphasized by the skimpy top and panties she was about to wear to bed.

A scrap of peach-colored material caught his eye and Gage braced off the door to investigate. He discovered the robe she was so obviously searching for. A light fragrance drifted from the satiny garment when he pulled it from beneath a bag on the armchair nearest the closet. He stole a moment to savor the feel of the material between his fingers. He let himself imagine how the item must feel with her filling it.

"Is this what you want?"

Alythia straightened, turning into his deep, close voice. She resisted the urge to let her lashes flutter out of embarrassment as she took what he offered.

"Thanks." Her tone was hushed as she slipped on the robe. "I probably shouldn't tell you I'm sorry about this, huh?"

His laughter was short but humor filled. "I can't think of one thing you have to be sorry for right now."

"Most men don't like to be teased." She reached for the ties at her waist.

Gage moved in, locating the other end of the belt. "Is that what you believed I'd think?" He secured the belt for her.

"I...shouldn't have said that."

Gage bumped her chin with his fist and then propped it there and waited for her eyes to meet his. "Will you answer me?"

"How could you *not* think that when all your friends have had their worlds rocked by all of mine?"

As impressed as he was that she had come right out and said it, Gage was still taken aback that she had. Her voice sounded strong, but he could sense that she was very exhausted. "Maybe it's a little early for this discussion?" he noted.

Exhaustion had indeed claimed the energetic lilt of her laughter. "*Never* is too early to have this discussion," she mused.

"If that's the case, I'm afraid we'll have to find something else to talk about over dinner."

"Another meal with the gang? Yaay." She gave a lazy twirl of an index finger. "What time do we need to be there?"

"*You and I* should be there around seven."

She blinked. "Just us? Just…you and me?"

"That's right." Gage realized he'd been rubbing the underside of her wrist where she had been holding her arms folded near where he still held on to the robe's belt.

"Seven?" he queried, smiling in a manner that proved he sensed both her reluctance and her willingness.

"Seven." She gave in to what she wanted. "What should I wear?"

Gage had a fine idea that his expression was probably all the response she needed. "I don't really think you'd benefit from my suggestion. It'd be a pretty self-serving one anyway."

The words made Alythia laugh until he gave the belt a sharp tug, which caused her to balance herself by bracing her hands against his unyielding chest when she jostled him. She dug in her fingers just enough to determine whether he felt as unbelievable as he appeared.

He dropped a kiss to the corner of her mouth. "Rest up," he murmured while his lips still grazed her skin.

Alythia stood fixed to her spot when Gage moved away. She watched him make his way out of the room. She maintained her position until a minute after the main door closed behind him.

What the hell was going on? The words blasted around inside her head, which must've had a stimulating effect, because she stripped off the robe. She let it lie where it fell and then eased beneath the inviting turned-down bedcovers.

She hadn't come here for this. She'd come for work and, if time permitted, a little lazing near the pool, a few drinks… She hadn't come here to fall in—

"Stop it." She punched the closest pillow as though it had somehow been to blame for such thoughts filling her mind. She barely had time for her friends. She surely had *no* time for a high-maintenance relationship.

Something told her that an involvement with Gage Vincent would be high maintenance. Not in a bad way, of course. She could, however, take one look at the man and be pretty much reassured that he'd keep her…busier than business ever could.

"Stop it…" She moaned the word as if begging herself for mercy.

Sex—or the lack of it—was the very last thing she needed at the forefront of her mind. The idea gave her pause and she ceased her fidgeting beneath the sheets. Giving in might not be such a bad thing after all. Well…

no, it wouldn't be a *bad* thing at all. Would it really matter what he thought of her later?

Chances were high that they wouldn't even see each other after the wedding. It'd just be a Caribbean fling. Who didn't deserve to have at least one of those? she thought, renewed drowsiness beginning to settle in as the perfect mattress and pillows cushioned her entire body, beckoning it into relaxation.

"No…a Caribbean fling wouldn't be a bad thing. He already wants you, Aly…" she murmured, the breeze and palm leaves lulling her as surely as the bed and its trimmings.

"And he'd really be a pleasure to…have…. Mmm…" She snuggled down almost into the center of the bed, thinking of those stunning eyes of his, the flawless coffee skin taut across that amazing chest.

A Caribbean fling wouldn't be a bad thing at all….

Chapter 5

Alythia's late-afternoon nap had worked wonders. The exhaustion that had threatened to buckle her knees when the plane had landed in San Juan had been effectively vanquished by the three-hour snooze. She awoke refreshed—and starving. The delicious and filling on-board lunch had worn off hours ago.

Thankfully, the hunger hadn't affected her appearance. She looked rested and stunning. She'd showered, dressed and then critiqued her image in the full-length mirror. Unless she was going out on the town, she rarely wore foundation. Her usual enhancement was a light dousing of eye shadow and lipstick. She'd packed a nice supply of all things makeup related but decided in that moment that they would remain packed. A healthy dose of sleep, rustling palm-tree leaves and a heavenly bed were the real secrets to radiance!

There was a knock and she felt a twinge of self-consciousness then. "Let's hope my date thinks so." She checked the gold-filigree clock on the dresser across the bedroom. She spared a minute for one last twirl in the mirror, loving the way the long hem of the lavender halter dress whirled around the flat sandals that highlighted her fresh pedicure. With one last quick toss of her blue-black waves, she headed for the door.

Had she had any concerns about whether Gage would disapprove of her joining him barefaced, she did away with them the instant she noticed the brilliant smile that set his gaze sparkling.

"You already answered my first question—did you sleep okay?" he asked with a striking grin. "Hungry?"

Alythia threw back her head as though she were depleted. "Starved, but sleep had to come first for me."

"Surprised that you got three uninterrupted hours of it." He leaned on the doorframe while voicing the observation.

"I still can't believe that, either." She blinked as if the remark gave her pause. "Did I miss anything…best left unmentioned?"

Gage bowed his head, studying his thumb as it traced the links of the silver timepiece he sported. "I think it's safe to say that everybody had a pretty quiet day." He pushed off the frame then, invading Alythia's space to course his hands over her bare arms.

"Got a wrap or anything?"

Gage's question went unanswered, his touch having rendered Alythia speechless and immovable for a weighty second. "I, um…" She motioned to the sofa, where a mosaic-print garment lay carelessly on a cushion. "Just there," she directed, thinking that he'd intended to collect it for her.

"Gage?" she called, tilting her head curiously when he only stood there smoothing his hands across her arms. "Hey?" She gave a tug to the cuff of the black shirt he wore outside cream-colored trousers.

"Right." He blinked and seemed to snap out of his reverie.

Alythia returned to the bedroom to grab her purse while Gage went to claim the wrap. She couldn't resist making another stop before the mirror to tousle her naturally windswept hair.

Gage was in possession of the wrap and had come to the bedroom door to watch her fussing in the mirror. Where the devil had she come from? He posed the question in silence but could still hear the bewilderment holding the words.

How was it he had never heard of her? He posed the second silent query and then caught himself. Heard of her? Exactly how up-to-date was he on any movers and shakers in the boutique business? Besides, Charlotte wasn't exactly a town where one saw his or her neighbors at the corner market on the regular. Still… what were the odds of meeting such a woman on a trip like this?

Such a woman? He considered that wording. Exactly what type of woman did he mean? He had a fine idea what type of women her friends were. He didn't hold that against them, but that wasn't Alythia.

She was very protective of her girls and he admired her for that. But was that all? Her looks and sexual appeal had captured him, there was no doubting that, but there was more. He believed that solving the mystery of her would simply ensnare him, happily entrap him far more than he already was.

Alythia offered up a sheepish smile when she turned from the mirror and found Gage staring. "Ready," she gushed, not reading the true intensity lurking in the liquid chocolate of his stare.

She reached for the wrap, but Gage held it out of her grasp, choosing to place it across her shoulders.

"You think I'll need this inside?" she asked.

"Doubt it." His response was canyon deep and absent.

Alythia didn't ask why he was draping it over her shoulders, then.

A good thing, too, because Gage wasn't sure she'd appreciate knowing that his reason was only that he wanted to touch her. The flat sandals were chic, sexy in a totally subtle way. She would most likely have been closer to his eye level were she wearing anything with a more substantial heel. Her lithe, fragile build beautifully enhanced the full B-cups and nicely rounded bottom that Gage was more than a little curious to discover the feel of cradled in his palms.

"Second thoughts?" she was asking, seeming curious about his fixed expression. She gave another light tug to his shirt cuff and smiled a bit brighter when he dipped his head to veil a suddenly bashful expression.

"Let's go." He cocked his head just slightly toward the door.

Quietly, they headed out.

Alythia was surprised to feel faint pinpricks of apprehension take hold. She knew what had stirred them but had no plan as to how to approach the subject.

"So where are we eating?" she asked instead.

"The resort's got a pretty good Italian restaurant. Um, loads of other stuff, too, if Italian's not…not your thing."

Uneasiness aside, Alythia couldn't help but smile over how concerned he seemed about making her aware that the choice was hers.

"You seem to know a lot about this place." She eased into the next phase of quelling her curiosity and satisfying those annoying pinpricks. "Must be nice to have a friend in the hospitality business."

They had arrived at the elevator bay. Gage had already pulled Alythia's arm into its usual place across the crook of his elbow. They walked the corridor, golden lit at night by the electric candles lining the walls. By day, rich sunlight was powerful enough to filter through the picture windows at either end of the space. Softly evocative tunes from the band on schedule for that evening piped in to enhance their stroll along the otherwise silent hall.

"Having a friend in the business is very nice but Dane, Zeke and Jay benefit more than I do." He depressed the elevator's down button and then hid his hand in a front trouser pocket. "My visits down here aren't usually about vacationing."

"Hmm…" Alythia tapped her fingers along the powerful cords of his forearm. "Sounds like *your* friends and *my* friends both have *workaholic* friends in common." She joined in for only a moment when Gage laughed to concede her point.

"Is that all the enjoyment you get from Clive's brainchild?" She ventured more steadily into the topic she had wanted to open since they left her suite.

"Clive doesn't complain." Gage shrugged. "Especially when my trips down here result in free business advice for him."

The elevator car arrived with a melodic and subtle ring.

"Does Clive only make moves you give the green light on?" Alythia asked once the doors closed and they began their descent.

Gage leaned against the rich oak-paneled car and regarded her with a fresh awareness. "Alythia?" He waited for her eyes to rest on his. "Clive isn't about to back out on this deal because of anything *I* say."

"I didn't mean—"

"Yes, you did." His words held no accusation, only soft amusement.

Sighing disappointedly, Aly lowered her eyes to the short carpeting beneath their feet. "Orchid's always warning me about being so anally involved in my business."

The close confines filled with the hearty rumble of Gage's laughter. "Do I even want to know what that is?" The question tumbled out on a chuckle.

The doors opened into the exotic music-filled lobby. Gage offered his arm, which Alythia accepted without thought.

"The explanation was forced on me," she said in a resigned fashion. "No reason why I can't share it with you."

Gage's ready laughter resumed as he led them deeper into the lively lobby.

"So I guess you finishing off our appetizers means you approve of the restaurant?" Gage drained the last of his beer and signaled the waiter for another.

Shameless, Aly scraped the last of the guacamole from a porcelain bowl. "It takes talent to make great guacamole and these folks have talent to spare."

"I'll have to make sure Clive keeps his cook staff, then."

There was a moment of quiet and then a flood of laughter between the couple as memories of their earlier conversation filtered in.

"So…anally involved in business?" Gage recalled the other path of their conversation before it had veered off into Alythia's ravings over Anegada Weeks' West Wing Restaurant Row.

The resort boasted over thirty eating establishments all along various wings inside the resort's main building. Each eatery carried a different theme and was staffed by Caribbean, Latin and Italian natives.

Alythia helped herself to more of the crisp sangria she'd ordered. Settling back, she studied the colorful liquid through the tall cooler she held.

"I prefer to think of it as being detail oriented. Orchid thinks I make a big deal of things when no big deal is required. It's a flaw I'm trying to work on." She shrugged and then drank deeply of the sangria.

Gage frowned. "I wouldn't say it's anything you need to stress over."

Aly held her glass poised in the air. "Excuse me? Are you the same man I just interrogated on the way down here?"

"I wouldn't have called it an interrogation."

"No…you're too polite to do that."

The assessment made him laugh again. Alythia didn't begrudge the attention he drew. Women turned in appreciation of the man and the sound of his amusement and Aly couldn't deny its ability to soothe.

"You don't know me very well." He sobered a bit. "Being detailed or *anally* involved is often a necessity in business. Those who aren't do so at the expense of their own interests."

"I see your point, but I think I could really stand to be a little less curious."

Gage tapped the base of the beer bottle while relaxing in his chair. "Questions aren't bad things, Alythia."

"Tell my friends that."

To himself Gage agreed that questions could prove pesky for anyone who lived as footloose as her girls— or *his* boys. "How often do you find yourself on the receiving end of their disapproval?" he asked.

Aly appeared stumped by the question but didn't have to locate an answer straightaway. The server had arrived with a fresh chilled beer for Gage and to take their entrée orders.

"You should try the sangria." Aly sang her words of encouragement.

"I'm good." Gage was pouring the brew into a tall frosted mug.

Aly was insistent. "If you try the sangria, I could order a pitcher instead of this inappropriate cooler."

"Order the pitcher, Alythia."

"And drink it by myself? Thanks for making *me* look like the lush."

"It's the Caribbean," he chuckled.

"It is, isn't it?" She reciprocated the waiter's smile. "A pitcher of sangria and bring *two* coolers, please. In case Mr. Vincent changes his mind."

"You know, I promise not to give you a hard time if you want to chug the damn thing right from the pitcher."

Aly threw back her head and laughed vibrantly. Gage propped his chin on his fist and simply enjoyed the sound of it. Each time he caught a glimpse of her eyes, he was struck by their amethyst shade and the enchanting way the light filtered through the almond-shaped orbs.

He thought she may have spied the intent way he watched her, because her laughter quieted a bit too abruptly. She seemed to withdraw a bit into herself. He didn't want to push, but he didn't care overmuch for the haunted look that had suddenly crept into her eyes.

"Alythia?"

"I love my friends, but they make me nervous." She blinked then, as though sharing the confession had all at once drawn her up and out of her thoughts.

"I can't believe I said that." She slapped her hands to her cheeks and watched Gage as if she was in awe. "You're a little *too* easy to talk to."

Gage leaned close to pull one hand down from her face. "I promise it goes no further than our table."

"I still shouldn't have said it."

"Don't you have a right to your opinion?" He gave a flip wave and reached for his chilled Samuel Adams. "My friends make me nervous all the time—I never know when I'll need to have bail money ready." He smirked. "But I guess they feel the same way about me. It's to be expected when it comes to friends, especially the wild and crazy ones." The smirk became a lopsided grin that was intended to make her smile.

Aly put forth a real effort, but clearly her heart wasn't in it. "It's not the same," she said.

"Because you're women?" he guessed.

The sangria arrived blessedly fast and Aly watched the rich red drink being poured as though she were a woman dying of thirst.

"Sir? Will you be joining your lady?" the server asked.

Alythia stopped the glass midway to her mouth. Her eyes clashed with Gage's and she looked away, desperate for something to focus on across the dining room.

Gage didn't appear at all displeased by the waiter's unintentional slip. "I'd very much like to join my lady."

"Yes…it's different because we're women." Aly waited to voice her agreement until after they'd taken a few sips of the sangria.

"Alythia—"

She waved off the apology he was about to utter. "Blame it on my stupid curiosity, but I really want to know what's going through your mind right now about my friends."

Gage set aside his cooler, losing his taste for the fruity drink. "Honey, I don't know 'em well enough to voice an opinion like that."

"Not even the bride? That's strange considering she's about to marry one of your best friends."

"Jay tends to live in his own world and has always had a problem with ridicule. Besides, he's kind of kept us all in the dark about this."

"Ah…so he'd expect some kind of ridicule if he'd shared things with you guys about Orchid?"

Gage made another stab at finishing his sangria. Silently, he complimented Alythia's sharp mind while simultaneously condemning his loose tongue.

"I promise that nothing you say here will go further than our table...." She smiled.

"What do you want to know?" He set the cooler down.

"I'd like to know what you think of my friends."

"And what's that got to do with why they make you nervous?"

"I'll make it easy for you," Aly countered, expertly sidestepping his question. "What do you think of them based on your impressions during the flight?"

Gage rested an elbow on the table. Tapping fingers against his brow, he let her glimpse his weariness. He couldn't see their conversation going anywhere but down. "I didn't bring you out for this," he said finally.

Aly shook the fruit at the bottom of her glass and shrugged. "I'm sure you didn't."

"That's not fair, Alythia."

"I'm not accusing you." She fixed him with a non-judgmental look. "You'd be well within rights to expect I'd follow in my friends' footsteps. I just think it's best to get it out of the way and tell you you're wasting your time with me if you expect that. I'm not made that way."

"Your dining requests are coming through just now."

The attentive server returned with the food update. Gage pushed back his chair and stood, drawing the waiter aside, where they conducted a brief and quiet chat.

Alythia watched Gage push a few bills into the man's shirt pocket, and then he was helping her from her chair and escorting her from the dining room.

Nerves mixed in with a considerable amount of regret, but Aly kept up with Gage's long strides out of

the restaurant. She could almost feel the waves of fury
he radiated. He surely had every right to be pissed, she
thought, recalling Orchid's consistent accusations about
her anal involvement in business. That was an inaccu-
rate summation. She was anally involved in friendship
drama, which always found a way to weave itself in and
make her a complete basket case.

Alythia decided not to waste time in trying to explain herself to him. She'd just accept the silent treat-
ment on the way back to her suite. At least he wasn't
too angry to walk her back. Then they could forget their
poor attempt at following their friends' dance steps to
the bedroom and get on with enjoying the rest of their
vacations separately.

It was then that Alythia discovered they weren't
headed back to the suites but out of the resort's main
hall entirely. Aly shivered as much from the chill of the
evening air kissing her bare skin through the wrap as
she did from the anticipation of what was to follow their
sudden departure from the dining room. Curiosity had
her close to bursting, but she pressed her lips together to
silence any questions that might have tried to slip past.

"Questions aren't bad, but there are occasions when
the timing is," he said from where he stood behind her
once they were on a deserted strip of the beach.

Regardless of what was in store for the remainder
of the evening, a portion of Alythia's unease did begin
to fade when the ocean's quiet roar reached her ears.
Awed, she moved as if tugged by some unseen force
toward the sound of the water. The surf was just visible
via the strong moonlight and a powerful glow radiated
along the rear expanse of the resort to douse the beach
with a mellow illumination.

Once again the sea air that had calmed her upon arrival so many hours earlier had the same effect as she inhaled it then. Even the rush of the waves bumping the shore induced a great degree of solace. She smiled when the cool water sluiced between her toes, gliding between the soles of her feet and her sandals.

Gage stood off to Aly's side several feet away and just outside the range of the seeking water. Head bowed, his hands were propped lightly at his lean hips.

"My friends make me nervous because they do things that other people expect me to do when I'm with them." She at last gave him the answer he wanted. "So much of me wants to be that way, free and without a care for the consequences, but I—I can never trust it and relax enough to… Part of me wonders if I just care too damn much about what people think of me or…maybe I just…" *Care too damn much about who I'm free with.* She could only share the last with herself.

"Jeena thinks I'm a Goody Two-Shoes." She laughed and then turned to Gage, who stared fixedly while she confided. "I know you hate apologies, but I really am sorry for ruining your night."

He regarded her for a few moments more, tracking his golden-chocolate gaze up and down her body. Slowly, he covered the distance between them. Smoothing his hands over her arms, he massaged her through the silken material of the wrap.

"You didn't ruin my night." The massage he applied to her arms served to draw her closer even as it pampered her.

"I wanted to have dinner, laugh and talk…not about this…." He joined in when she laughed. "My night was about as far from ruined as it could get."

His head dipped and he plied her with what was intended to be a peck. That peck turned into something worthy of residing in the realm of full-blown lust. In the back of her mind, Aly remembered what she'd said about not being able to relax enough. That was a myth that Gage Vincent was effectively demolishing as his tongue enticed hers into a lazy duel.

The act progressed, slowly at first, as though Gage was more intent on exploring than taking. He stroked the roof of her mouth, crested his tongue along the ridge of her teeth before returning to play with her tongue. He evaded when she would have engaged and chuckled when she whimpered her impatience at his tactics.

Aly wouldn't, couldn't, stop to consider what type of mixed signal she might have been giving him. After all, she'd just claimed that she could never relax enough to be free, only to turn around and kiss him senseless. She didn't care what he thought in that moment, only that he kept doing what he was doing.

Alythia hadn't given thought to how hungry she was for affection until it was being oh so incredibly given to her. She reciprocated the suckling intensity he treated her to when he had her tongue entangled with his. She planned to give and take for as long as she could.

Or until the sound of glasses, dinnerware and cutlery filtered through her erotically charged thoughts. Alythia sighed her disappointment when Gage patted her hip, easing her out of the kiss as he did so.

Opening her eyes, Aly immediately searched for the source of the sounds that had interrupted her romantic moment beneath tropical stars. Blinking owlishly, she frowned at the sight a few yards from where she and

Gage stood. There was a table set for a candlelight meal for two. She looked to him.

Gage slanted her a wink. "Dinner is served."

Chapter 6

Dinner looked amazing and she was in fact starving. Alythia was, however, willing to let her stomach take a backseat to her… She wouldn't finish the thought. Not even silently. Instead, she tried putting on a gracious look, yet felt her facial muscles failing her miserably.

"Clive sure does pull out all the stops for his friends," she noted as they neared the beautifully set table. "At least *you've* got friends who offer less stress than they give."

"You didn't know him in college." Gage grinned, then sobered a bit. "Clive's a good guy." He rounded the table after pushing in her chair and looked to be debating his next words. "He's ethical, too. You can believe me when I say that he'd never accept or back out of a deal because of anything I or anyone else might say."

Alythia shook her head, hitting her cheeks with a

few wavy locks. "I shouldn't have said that, assumed that he was—"

"What? Like most of the men you've done business with?"

"Ha! No…no, actually, I've been fortunate enough to deal with mostly women in my business so far."

"Glad to hear it."

Alythia was wincing. "That didn't sound quite so cold in my head."

"I'm still glad to hear it. If your effect on Clive is any example, you'd probably have more men than him falling in love with you."

"In love?" she said with a laugh, and then reached down to unfasten and remove her sandals. "He sure is easy to please. We haven't even had a real conversation in person yet."

"The man's been known to fall in love during a phone call, so…" Gage provided a noncommittal shrug.

The couple indulged in a round of laughter at Clive's expense. Gage was the first to sober and had more fun watching Alythia succumb to another bout of mirth. His laughter had curbed into a smile as he shifted, reclining comfortably in his seat, and watched her. He'd wanted to kiss her since he saw her, wanted to know if her mouth was as soft as it looked and if her tongue felt as sweet as the words it formed sounded.

He shifted again, realizing that his *wants* were starting to affect parts of his body best left settled.

"Bless you," Alythia was saying as the servers set dinner in place. She had ordered a petite sirloin with scallops and au gratin potatoes.

Chef salad and rolls served as the table's centerpiece.

Gage indulged in a heartier New York strip, his side portions just a tad larger than Alythia's. They dined in companionable silence, which was marked only by the sound of waves and the faint vibration of music. The grooves bumped from either the resort's main building or the beachfront bar a ways down the shore—it was hard to tell which. Nevertheless, the sounds were a perfect accompaniment to a delicious meal.

The sounds *were* a perfect accompaniment to a delicious meal until they were marred by the unmistakable undercurrents of argument. Gage caught the voices before Alythia did. She heard him curse and looked up and back over her shoulder, closing her eyes at the sight of Jeena and Zeke.

The couple stormed down the beach, their bodies turning slightly inward as they spoke what appeared to be increasingly heated words the closer they came to where Gage and Alythia dined.

Zeke and Jeena had yet to notice their friends eating a few yards away, but their voices were well within range. Alythia bowed her head, feeling the sting of the words Zeke directed at her friend as though they were being aimed at her.

"Such a joke," he spat. "Do you know how stupid you sound talking about healthcare plans for a bunch of hookers?"

Jeena was tough to the bone. Alythia knew she'd refuse to cower or cry regardless of how deep the words cut.

"At least it's something *I* built! I don't have to sponge money off of a more successful friend to scratch out a little *piece* of something like that pitiful brokerage firm of yours! How many gasps of air has it taken this week?"

The lovers' spat went back and forth. Aly, though reluctant to do so, finally sent a look over to Gage. He appeared as beleaguered as she felt.

Gage shook his head. *I'm sorry,* he mouthed.

Aly's smile almost turned into a grin. It seemed that the phrase had become a staple of their brief acquaintance. Jeena's and Zeke's voices raised another octave then.

"I was so wrong about you!"

"Then we're a perfect mixed match!" Zeke threw up his hands. "'Cause I was exactly *right* about you! Guess a person really is what they do for a living. Least I didn't have to pay for it!"

Whatever toughness Jeena claimed dissolved. Then she was running, stumbling along the stretch of beach away from Zeke, Gage and Alythia.

"Jeena!" Aly scrambled from the table to call out to her friend. It was no good. She looked to Gage.

"I should go see about her." She sent a regretful look toward her half-finished meal.

"Go." Gage waved a hand.

Aly hesitated another few seconds, then backed away from the table and turned to race down the shore, kicking up tufts of sand as she went after Jeena. She'd bypassed Zeke, who was extending his hands as though he was about to plead his case.

Zeke let his hands fall to his sides in an "oh well" gesture. He turned, giving a start as though he'd just realized Gage was there.

"G!" Easy and lighthearted at once, Zeke gave an

approving smile at the table. He took a seat in the chair Aly had just vacated.

"Looks good!" he raved. Sniffing at a glass, he realized it was water and tossed the liquid to the sand in order to refill the glass with the wine left chilling in the bucket near the table.

Defeated, Gage resumed his seat and rested his forehead in his palm.

"Thanks for letting me ramble on so late or so early in the morning. What time is it there?"

Marianne yawned through the phone line. "Too early to try and get my eyes to focus in on a clock."

Aly smiled. "Thanks anyway."

"What you pay me for, hon."

"Not exactly." Aly rubbed at her temple. "I don't pay you to listen to stupid tales of drama featuring me and my friends."

"Well…if it affects your well-being, it *is* my business, so it's all good."

"Get some rest, Mari. You've earned it. We'll talk later."

"*Much* later. Can you at least try and take *one* day for yourself?"

"I'll try." Aly hoped that wouldn't turn out to be a lie and ended the call. She set aside the phone and returned her attention to the view from where she sat in one of the cushioned bamboo chairs along the balcony.

The suite was dark. She hadn't bothered with the lights after returning from Jeena's room. It hadn't been easy, but she'd finally gotten her friend settled enough to get some sleep. Too wired to sleep herself, Aly had decided to call Marianne, to whom she had been venting for the past forty-five minutes.

Aly checked her mobile for the time and figured she'd best *try* to get a little sleep herself if she hoped to appear halfway among the land of the living when she met with Clive Weeks later that day.

On perfect cue the doorbell rang. *No more.* Alythia dropped her face in her palms to muffle the sound.

The bell was followed by knocking and Aly heard her name on Gage's voice. After a second's hesitation she left the chair and padded through the living area. Her forced smile was an appropriate match to his concerned one when she opened the door.

"You okay?" he asked.

She could only nod, a gesture that ceased when Gage moved closer to rest against the doorframe.

"Did you eat?" His gaze seemed to intensify tenfold as he peered down at her.

Aly laughed abruptly, looking bewildered, as though she couldn't imagine where she found strength to fuel the reaction.

"I managed to convince Jeena to have some soup. I took some for myself but it was a far cry from the dinner I didn't get to finish."

"How's Jeena?"

Aly could only shake her head.

Gage provided a weak smile. "I could always apologize."

She backed away from the door as though he'd told her he had a plague. "Could we please find another phrase to put in place of 'I apologize' or 'I'm sorry'?"

Gage lifted his thumb to the corner of his mouth and appeared to be debating. "How about 'That's too bad'?"

"Sold!" She was surprised by the honest ripple of laughter she gave.

"I think my suggestion should come with a peace offering."

Aly saw the straps of her sandals dangling from his index and middle fingers. "Hmph, good thing I didn't get more comfortable."

"Mmm-hmm." Whatever interest Gage had in talking seemed to have vanished, for he suddenly pushed off the doorframe and advanced.

Alythia had opened her mouth to thank him for returning her shoes but he never gave her the chance. For the second time that day, her body reacted to the delicious sensation of his mouth on hers. Again he began with a tentative exploration that quickly blossomed into a sensuous entwining of their tongues.

Gage withdrew from the kiss to outline the curve of her cheek, brush the sensitive skin behind her ear and trail his nose along her neck.

"Gage?"

"Mmm…"

"Do you kiss all women you know so soon after you meet them?"

He nipped at her earlobe. "Would you believe that I've forgotten every other woman I've ever met?"

"No," she gasped, still enraptured by his touch and feeling the vibration of laughter through his body.

"You really know how to hurt a man."

"It's not out of habit." Aly felt her sandals bumping her bottom when he switched them to his other hand while he held her. "So what do I have to do to get my shoes back?" she murmured against his jaw, wanting his mouth on hers.

Something in Alythia's question, however, cooled Gage's ardor, for he rested his forehead on her shoulder as if he was suddenly drained. He straightened.

"You don't have to do one thing." He glanced around the living area, grimacing slightly, as though he was displeased with himself.

"I'll…um…I'll let you get some rest." He retreated to the door.

"Okay…." Her agreement was at odds with the questions and confusion clouding her mind. Had she said—done—something wrong?

Gage offered the sandals and she hoped her efforts to mask disappointment were good enough. Aly took special care not to let her fingers touch his hands when she took the shoes.

"Thanks." She didn't bother to show him to the door and he left without a look back.

"Is this only day *two* of our *fantastic* Caribbean getaway?" Jeena moaned, holding her head in her hands while she and Alythia took in the beach view from Jeena's balcony later that morning.

They had ordered breakfast for Orchid and Myrna, who were on the way to join them. Aly enjoyed the breeze and shade while relaxing in one of the lounge chairs surrounding the squat glass table that carried their breakfast fixings—fruit, biscuits, cheeses, turkey bacon and sausage, and a bowl of breakfast potatoes. Matching tea- and coffeepots were the table's centerpieces.

"You should eat," Alythia ordered from beneath the wide brim of a floppy straw hat. She risked taking a peek at Jeena, smiling when the woman pouted for a moment longer, then delved into the filling meal.

Aly took on greeting responsibilities when she heard the faint chime of the doorbell. She found the last two members of her crew on the other side.

"Long time no see," Myrna drawled, tugging Aly into a hug.

Orchid had no time for such pleasantries. She'd already pushed her way past Aly and Myrna and was headed to the balcony.

"What the hell did you say to Zeke?" she demanded of Jeena.

"Dammit." Alythia rolled her eyes toward Myrna. "I just got Jeen to calm down. This is the last thing they need to be talking about."

"You can forget that," Myrna countered while they speed-walked to the balcony. "Zeke was bitchin' to Jay about it pretty much all night. Ork's not in much of a 'benefit of the doubt' frame of mind."

Aly stumbled to a halt. "How do you know that?"

"Oh, Dane and I stopped by their room before we went back to ours."

Alythia delivered a quick prayer that the falling-out sure to occur when Dane relieved Myrna of the notion that they were a couple would wait until after things settled with Zeke and Jeena.

Or *Orchid* and Jeena, as it were. Aly arrived out on the balcony to find her oldest friends squared off in the middle of a shouting match.

"How can you take that jackass's side over mine!"

"Because I've heard it all before! You always get upset when somebody tells you the truth about what you do for a living!"

"Orchid—"

"Passing yourself off like some kind of business-woman." Orchid ignored Alythia's attempt to interrupt. "All you are is a pimp."

Myrna gasped.

"Bitch," Jeena spat. "I'd rather be a pimp than a slut. At least a hooker gets paid."

Orchid winced as though the words were a physical blow. "What are you tryin' to say?"

"You never were very bright, were you?" Jeena sneered, folding her arms over the red robe she'd thrown on over matching pjs. "Then again, you never had to be, with Aly in your corner."

"Don't even try it! Y'all are *not* drawin' me into this!"

The women didn't seem to notice Aly bolting from the balcony.

"Aly to make you seem smarter than you are, your family's money to make you seem more respectable that you could ever hope to be and a parade of idiots in your bed to solidify your slut status!" Jeena wailed. The wind whipped her short hair about her face and added to the wild aura she cast.

Impossibly, the voice volume continued to heighten. In the living room, Aly could only hope the women wouldn't come to blows. As she was on her way out, Myrna would indeed ruin her manicure trying to break them apart.

"You're crazy, Alythia Marie Duffy, if you think you're leavin' *me* here with them fools," Myrna hissed when she raced out into the living room behind Aly.

"It's okay, Mur, I already called Jay to come get his fiancée." Alythia patted a side pocket on her rust-colored shirtdress to ensure her room key was inside. "You only have to keep the peace for a few more minutes. If you get nervous, call Dane."

"And where are *you* going?" Myrna propped her hands, fingers-down, on her hips.

"I have a meeting." Alythia sighed in relief, not seeing the need to hide her motives any longer.

Myrna straightened, her cool, lovely gaze narrowing with discovery. "That's why you came on the trip, isn't it?"

"And it's a good thing, too. At least I'll get something out of it besides catfights."

Myrna glanced in the general direction of the balcony. "Don't you even care enough to help me calm them down?"

"Please, Mur, Jeena will see what an idiot she was to have sex with that horse's ass thirty minutes after she met him."

Myrna blinked. "Is that what you think about me and Dane?"

"Sweetie, you and Dane are *not* a couple." Aly's tone was full of sympathy but she wouldn't apologize for her honesty.

"You're wrong. We've been talking and we plan to keep on seeing each other when we get back."

"I'm sure you will. He's not ready to close off a new sex pipeline so fast."

"You take that back!"

"Ah, Myrna, do you hear how childish you sound?" Aly clasped her hands in a pleading gesture against the front of her dress. "Y'all have been ridiculous with these guys."

"Well, Aly, maybe me and Jeen want to find what Orchid has! Unlike *you,* maybe *we* don't want to wind up lonely with only a bank account to show for a long life."

"Mur." Alythia's expression was one of sudden suspicion. "You don't think Dane's gonna marry you?" She could see in Myrna's eyes that she held on to just that hope. "Sweetie, you and Jeen are just something they wanted to play with for a while."

Myrna was shaking her head. "Do you ever get sick of being so upstanding? So high, mighty and right all the damn time?"

"I'm sorry you think that, Mur. I don't mean to hurt you. It's just so clear what's happening. I'm just sorry you guys can't see it."

"Go to your meeting, Aly." Myrna smirked. "Business is the only thing you'll probably ever get off on anyway."

Alythia watched Myrna head back into the argument on the balcony. Her fingers ached with the need to pull the woman back, hug her and try to work it out. She resisted, for the first time feeling that a permanent line was being marked between her and her dearest friends.

Chapter 7

The Weeks' Resort Outlet Lane had all the quaint charm of a Mediterranean village. The cobblestone streets and stone structures seemed right at home amid the tropical loveliness of Anegada. Partially hidden by the lush palm tree leaves, the area gave its visitors the revitalizing feel of stepping into a world long past.

Alythia judged from the number of resort guests she saw inside and along the streets of the shopping village that such an effect was most probably quite successful in opening wallets and purses.

"I could see it," she announced to no one in particular, and heard soft chuckling afterward. Turning, she saw that Clive Weeks was the culprit.

"May I take your reaction to mean that we'll be doing business?" she asked.

"Only if your business manager agrees."

"She's fired if she doesn't."

They shared a laugh.

"She'll agree based on the location alone." Aly sobered a little and took closer inventory of her surroundings. "That way she can delude herself into believing her workaholic client is at least a *little* distracted from business."

Clive pretended to be crestfallen. "So the place would only distract you a *little?*"

"Well, I wouldn't want her to think I was *completely* falling down on the job." Her shrug was as playful as her smile.

"Well, you already know what *my* business manager thinks." Clive folded his arms over the pale blue shirt he wore and relaxed against the framing along the glass doors at the back of the proposed retail space for the boutique.

Alythia continued to walk in slow circles, assessing the area and conjuring promotional ideas. "And what about you? Do you really believe a clothing store would fare well here?"

"Are you kidding? I'm surprised I didn't have the idea sooner."

"Well, maybe the right idea hadn't come along yet."

"Yeah…" Clive's playfully crestfallen look returned. "Now I've got the right idea—and a woman after my own heart, if only my friend hadn't met you first."

Alythia took no offense to the teasing gibe, though a curious element crept over her expression. "Your interest in the boutique now wouldn't all be part of a favor you're doing for that friend, would it?"

Clive moved from the doorframe, a wave of seriousness having claimed him, as well. "The idea appealed to me so much I wasn't sure whether to trust it, so I asked Gage for his opinion." His guileless grin returned. "I'm happy he agreed, otherwise I'd have had to go against one of the best minds in business."

"You won't be sorry about this, Clive."

"I know." He rubbed his hands together and looked around the snug, sunny space. "I think I'll give you time alone to get acclimated to the place."

"Sounds good." She took both his hands and shook them as enthusiastically as he did hers. "Thanks, Clive."

He left her with a wink and a nod. Alythia waited for him to disappear down an overgrown side road and, after making sure there were no other prying eyes, broke into a carefree dance around the space. She stopped short then, recalling her talk with Myrna earlier that morning. Business wasn't all she could *get off* on, but it would have to do for a while longer.

Though smaller than her other two locations, the Anegada space boasted large picture windows to the front and rear of the main floor. There would be perfect natural lighting during the day and a lovely view of twinkling lights from the resort at night. Alythia made a note to return one evening to see the effect for herself.

Beyond the double glass doors, the rear exit opened out into a small courtyard and offered a striking view of the beach. Dropping down to one of the lounges, Alythia envisioned daily fashion shows in the space to entice patrons inside for a closer look.

Aly pressed her head back into the navy-and-gray lounge cushions and commanded her brain to take a break. Her business was pretty much concluded, then, and it was time for a retreat from all things dramatic and confusing.

Gage Vincent came to mind then. Confusing? No, he was pretty much laying it all on the line about what he wanted. Wasn't he? She thought about his behavior when he'd come to check on her after Jeena's battle with Zeke. Maybe he'd decided to call it quits before anything really got started between the two of them. She certainly couldn't blame him in light of the drama he had been witness to courtesy of her friends.

But that wasn't quite fair, was it? What about *his* friends and their behavior? Couldn't she just as easily back away from him in light of what *she'd* been witness to?

"Mmm… Aly, it's too early in the day for all this heavy thinking." Besides, she'd done enough of that with Clive. Satisfied, she rested with her eyes closed while she inhaled the floral air and treated her ears to the sounds of rushing water, wind and birdsong.

"Looks like Clive made a sale…."

Smiling, Alythia added the sound of Gage's voice to her list of soothing elements. "You bet he did. I'm gonna hire people to run the shop and just spend my days out here."

Gage took a seat on one of the accompanying lounges. "Sounds like the workaholic's getting tired of working so hard?"

"Can you blame me?" Aly took a long, indulgent stretch. "Honestly? Who could think of working with a view like this?"

Tell me about it. Gage knew the view he had in mind had nothing to do with the sand and waves. He could have watched her all day but the watching would definitely lead to a desire to touch and that was what causing all the…issues that were presently revealing themselves. Wouldn't she expect him to fall in line with his friends and make a play for her? Hadn't he done that already? They'd kissed more than once and she'd seemed to enjoy it as much as he had. Was there any more to it? he wondered.

The only thing he was sure of was that he didn't want to stop seeing her after the trip. Problem was, she might not be so interested if *his* friends and *her* friends kept butting heads. If he took her to his bed only to have things go awry… A voice chimed that at least he'd have had the pleasure of her in his bed. He lost himself in a study of the length and shapeliness of her legs bared beneath the knee-length hem of her dress. He finally tuned in that she was calling out to him and he saw her watching him inquisitively.

"Will you come dancing with me tonight?" He roamed the length of her legs again. "I planned for us to do that last night but, well…"

"We didn't even get through the eating part of our date," Aly laughed. "Do you really want to test fate again?"

"I'm willing." Gage leaned forward, resting his elbows on the khaki shorts covering his thighs. "I promise you'll have a good time if you let me show you one."

"I could use one." Alythia pushed a hand through her hair, held it there. "I could use a lot of things—another nap, breakfast…"

"You didn't have anything?"

Her smile was sad. "Breakfast with the girls got a little out of hand."

"Yeah…" Gage slumped back against his lounge, tossing a leg on either side and planting feet adorned in Crocs in the sand. "Jay came down on Orchid pretty hard last night."

"He did?" She pushed herself up to prop on an elbow and watch him expectantly. "Maybe that's why she came down so hard on Jeen this morning. Myrna must've missed Jay getting on her case about it last night when she and Dane stopped by. She said Ork didn't have much sympathy for our friend."

"That part's true." Gage tented his fingers above his abdomen, intermittently bumping them. "How much do you know about their relationship—Jay and Orchid's?"

"Not much." Aly rested back on the lounge. "Just what I told you before. It was all very sudden. What, um…what do you know?" she asked hesitantly.

"The wedding's for show, Alythia." He closed his eyes for a moment or two. "To secure some deal between Jay's family and hers."

"That's insane! Orchid wouldn't even go for something like that. Do families still even do that?"

"You'd be surprised how well a company's stock can do by a good run in the press. Everyone loves a wedding." He gave Aly a resigned smile. "It's all for show. According to Jay, Orchid's father threatened to cut her off if she balks."

"My God…" Aly was sitting up straight in the middle of the lounge, hand over her mouth.

"It's probably a good idea to keep this to yourself. Jay only told me after Orchid went to bed and Zeke left with Dane and Myrna."

"That explains all the overwhelming affection…." Aly shook her head, still incredulous. "And why she's so hell-bent on everybody getting along."

Gage watched Alythia cradle her head in her hands,

the wind whipping her hair into disarray. The last thing he'd wanted was to upset her.

"Let's get you some breakfast," he suggested.

"My appetite is suddenly gone."

"Then let's find it." He stood, offering a hand, and pulled her from the lounge when she accepted.

"I could just get room service." She slapped her hands to her sides. "Turn in after I eat."

"I don't trust you to do that." He reciprocated her gesture. "I do trust that I'll get you to eat and then put you to bed myself."

She rested a hand against the white tee he wore beneath an unbuttoned denim shirt. "Are you trying to save me, Gage Vincent?"

"No." He pulled her arm through his. "But I do like taking care of you."

Together they left the courtyard.

The Glow was located along the wing that housed the resort's bars and dance halls. Gage and Alythia had planned to meet there instead of him picking her up at the suite.

Aly didn't see her date right away and took a trip to the bar for a drink—*one* drink. While more would be enjoyable, it wasn't advisable. Besides, the early nap following lunch in the breakfast café located in the shopping villa had really hit the spot.

Aly had barely taken a sip of her piña colada when a man who had taken the seat next to her at the bar offered her another round.

"You should move on, sir. The lady isn't alone," the barkeep advised. He waited for the suitor to relinquish his seat and then acknowledged Alythia's curious stare.

"Mr. V's on his way, miss." He nodded.

Rather dazed, Aly turned on the barstool to see that Gage was in fact making his way through a moderately heavy crowd. His expression was unreadable even though he pulled many hungry looks from single and attached patrons.

His handsome face brightened when he saw her waiting. "Thanks for not standing me up," he teased.

"No problem." She shrugged. "My other options weren't very appealing."

"That's good to hear." He grinned, fingering one of the silver tassels dangling from the capped sleeves of her flare-legged powder-blue jumpsuit.

"Mr. V." The barkeep provided Gage with a drink.

"Wow, that's some gift. You didn't even tell him what you wanted." Aly propped her chin on her palm and watched Gage take a swig of a Samuel Adams brew. "Or is it that you've been here so often that everyone knows your favorite drinks?"

"Li'l bit of both," he said, throwing her a wink.

"Bartenders looking out for your drinks, your date… Nice. He practically kicked out this poor guy who tried to buy me a drink…." She trailed off, having captured a glimpse of a muscle flexing wickedly along Gage's jaw.

"Boyd was just looking out for *you,* actually." He cast a disapproving look around the bar. "Some places in Clive's resort can be…a challenge for a woman on her own."

"In what way?" Aly smiled when another barkeep provided her with a fresh drink.

"Usual." He shrugged. "Same as with any other club—drinks spiked with more than extra alcohol, for instance."

Aly gave her glass a cautious nudge. "Does that happen a lot?"

"Enough so that it's a concern for Clive." Gage turned to lean back against the bar and observe the establishment more fully. "The staff's on high alert when they see a gorgeous woman on her own at the bar."

"I see." Aly sipped her drink and then smiled. "And what if the gorgeous woman is the one doing the spiking?"

Her question roused Gage's laughter and Alythia soon joined in.

"That *would* be interesting," he said. "I honestly have no comeback for that."

"I'll bet." Aly laughed into her glass.

Gage extended his hand. "Maybe I'll think of something while we dance."

Playful skepticism brightened her expression. "Do you really think I can be trusted?"

His warm stare made a quick heated dip to the subtle V-cut bodice of her suit when he invaded her space a little more. "I'll trust you if you trust me. How's that?"

"I don't know.... I still think you're dangerous." Her playfulness curbed when she noted the change in his eyes.

"I believe I've been a very good boy." Again he toyed with the tassels at her sleeves. "Compared to some," he added.

"That's what makes you so dangerous." She tilted her head, lashes fluttering slightly against his whisper-soft touch. "You've got uncanny control over your restraint."

Gage nodded as though her point hadn't surprised him. "You know, that's what I used to think."

They were close then. Alythia was without word or

the ability to even produce one. She felt him squeezing her upper arm, patting her hip as he did so.

"How 'bout that dance?"

"That's what we're here for." She eased down off the barstool.

Gage acknowledged the truth in his words moments into the dance. Yes, the restraint he'd once prided himself on having was in fact gone, but the realization of that forced another question. How much restraint had he ever *truly* had?

His methods were—at least, he *hoped* they were— more refined than his friends'. Nonetheless, when it came to women, those methods were all meant to achieve the same goal: a new woman in his bed. Alythia Duffy was a beauty, no doubt, but beauty was what he tended to surround himself with. While her looks were what had first and shallowly beckoned him, they weren't his primary thoughts when she came to mind.

So what was it, then? Her concern for her friends? Dedication to her job? Or was his attraction more selfish— more about what she made him feel when he was in her presence?

What Aly felt then was calm, a stillness that had rooted itself someplace deep and was not budging. The music, while lovely and soothing, barely registered. She didn't care if her stance, pliant and clingy, unnerved him. She planned to enjoy the moment, indulge in every bit of what he was making her feel.

And how far was she willing to go in her desire to indulge? She inhaled from where her face rested in the side of his neck. Subtly, she arched, binding herself into his impressively athletic frame. She craved just a bit more of the incredible pleasure that his closeness provided.

Gage released her hand, which he'd curved into his chest. Then he was smoothing his palms across her back and shoulders. He massaged them down again, cupping her hips and enfolding them to bring her closer and seal her in the circle of his arms.

Somewhere the faint sound of shattering glass cluttered the air but the effect had no sway over the oasis sheltering them.

"Alythia..."

"Mmm..."

He brushed a kiss to her earlobe, gave it a dry suckle before applying the same attention to the sensitive skin beneath. "Will you think less of me if I ask you to come to bed with me?"

"Hmph." Her response was more of a sigh. "Will you think less of me if I accept?"

He straightened his stance then, curving a hand around the base of her throat. He kissed her hungrily, and she responded with equal fire, thrusting her tongue against his, rotating and stroking as if she was desperate for the friction.

Alythia heard a gasp, understandable. Kissing the man was a definite treat with the power to send tingles to every nerve ending she owned. The only problem was that the gasp hadn't come from her and had sounded more outraged than...sensual.

Sounds of a commotion had followed the shattering glass, at last encroaching upon the sweet oasis Gage and Alythia had enjoyed.

"They've got to be doing this stuff on purpose," he

murmured when he and Aly emerged from passion's sweet spell to discover that their mutual friends were at the center of a lovers' spat.

"No…" Aly groaned. She felt Gage take her chin and squeeze.

"Come with me," he encouraged when her bright eyes met his warm chocolate ones. "We really don't need to be here, do we?"

His question was answered by Myrna Fisher.

"Flaky backstabber!"

Dane Spears wasn't offended. "You should be happy to get rid of me. This place has lots more fools to screw and pretend they're your man."

Myrna responded by throwing a sticky mixed drink in his face and shoving his chest before she stormed out.

"We don't need to be here, but we probably should be," Aly said.

Gage kept her near when she attempted to move from his side. "One day I hope to have a friend as good as you."

Alythia closed her eyes and smiled. "Me, too."

Then she was gone. Gage's soft expression vanished the moment she moved through the chaotic crowd to reach Myrna.

A storm brewed in Gage's striking stare as he went to seek out his friend.

Alythia caught up to her girlfriend just as she approached the elevator corridor. Thankfully, the area was deserted. Myrna was so upset that Alythia didn't have to probe her for details. Myrna shared it all in a stream of anger and pain. She told her that the man of her dreams had slept with someone else.

"The masseuse, of all people! I'm such an idiot."
Myrna punched the up arrow on the elevator's panel.
"I thought it'd be fun to have a couple's massage. Dane
decided to spend half his time in the sauna. He didn't
spend it there alone."

Alythia reached out. "I'm sorry."

Myrna shrugged off Aly's hand when it touched her
shoulder. "Go on and tell me you told me so. I just want
to get the hell out of here." She punched the up arrow
again. "Forget this getaway, get-to-know-you—whatever
the devil it is."

"Mur." Aly stifled her instinct to move closer. "You
can't do that. Orchid's really counting on us right now.
It's really important to her." She pressed her lips together, annoyed that she couldn't explain the particulars
of *why* it was so important to their friend.

Myrna slowly turned from the elevator to fix Aly
with a scathing look. "Do you ever get sick of being
such a hypocrite?"

"Mur—"

"So it's okay for *you* to traipse off to handle business
when our friends need us, but I can't leave even after
I've just been humiliated?"

"Honey, I didn't mean it that way." Aly rubbed at
her temples.

Myrna snorted. "Yeah, right." She turned back to
the elevator.

Losing whatever patience she'd thought she had, Aly
flinched and then drew her hands from her face and
gave a resounding clap. "You know what? Do whatever the hell you want—you will anyway. Do you really think Dane Spears came here to find a soul mate?"
She laughed the words. "He didn't care a bit more about

that than any of the other dozens of guys you've taken to bed hoping they'd put a ring on your finger the next morning. Open your eyes, Mur. You're better than this."

Myrna had turned from the elevator again and still regarded Alythia coolly. "Since we're giving advice, Aly, I should tell you to keep your eyes open, too." She moved closer, ignoring the elevator car that arrived just then. "If you think that Gage Vincent is such a golden boy because he hasn't taken you to bed just yet, you can think again. From what I hear, that one loses interest very fast once he's gotten the panties and the fact that he hasn't taken yours yet isn't a token of how good he is." Myrna gave her a sulky once-over. "He's just trying to make it last. We *are* gonna be here for nine more days, you know?"

"Let me guess." Aly brought her hands to her hips. "Your soul mate told you this?"

Myrna stiffened but she didn't cower. "Just because you've got your face stuck in spreadsheets and faxes all day doesn't mean the rest of us don't have a clue about what's going on. Charlotte is still a small place. People talk—even about men as powerful and discreet as the great Gage Vincent." She left Alythia with another quick once-over and then turned. "You have a good night, Aly," she threw over her shoulder, and then disappeared inside an elevator that opened at the end of the bay.

Chapter 8

"An entire day, boss? Nice. I was up yesterday at six a.m. waiting for your call."

Gage forced a smile at Webb's tease. "Sorry I disappointed you."

"Pleased by your progress, sir," Webb Reese raved, and then cleared his throat noisily. "I hope you're in the mood for discussion, 'cause I'd love to know which way you'd lean on this bid thing."

"Nice try." Gage celebrated his urge to chuckle. "I only called to see if you were in any state of mind to answer your phone. Things must be going pretty well if you're able to manage that."

The sound Webb returned then was a cross between weariness and amusement. "Deciding this stuff is murder. Folks act like they'd either kill or sign over their firstborn to win out."

"It's not a game for the fainthearted." Gage shifted in the chair he occupied on the patio. "But if it helps, I always find it a good practice to carefully view all the information at hand and then just go with your gut."

Webb forced out another weary chuckle. "Going with my gut could be dangerous. Especially when the rest of my body's weighing in on it."

"Being propositioned already, huh?" Gage sipped OJ to muffle his laughter. "Webb, I'm impressed."

"Hmph. Thanks, sir, but it's nothing like that. Unfortunately."

Gage continued to chuckle.

"Some of the women are real go-getters, though," Webb mused. "I've yet to be so unforgettably propositioned, but I'm sure there are some who might not be against the idea."

"Welcome to the world of big business. Just remember that your head—the one on your shoulders—and your gut are the only body parts you need to consult with to get the job done."

Laughter then flooded both ends of the phone line.

Alythia had planned to spend the day on her own before she remembered that Orchid had arranged for the group to have breakfast together that morning. She'd spent half the night debating on doing exactly what she'd told Myrna she *couldn't* do. Hypocrite indeed, she acknowledged.

Still, accepting that the trip had been a bad idea and booking a ticket on the first flight out of paradise seemed like a fine decision. As bad as things had already gotten in the two days they'd been there, Aly couldn't help but believe they were going to get even worse and she couldn't put a finger on exactly how. She could only hope that the next uproar wouldn't be between her and Gage. They certainly hadn't spent much time together. Perhaps that would work in their favor and keep them away from each other's throats.

Yet that was just where she remembered being the night before, her face cuddled into his neck as they danced. He had asked her to come to bed with him.

Alythia stopped just short of the patio reserved for the group's breakfast. Gage had been the first to arrive and she watched him chuckling into the phone at his ear. He'd asked her to come to bed with him…and she'd accepted. She'd so wanted to go with him. Still did.

That one loses interest very fast once he's gotten the panties.

So what? she reasoned. They had only nine more days counting that one and she certainly wasn't looking for the soul mate Myrna had hoped to find.

Gage was done with the call and dropped his mobile to the rectangular table covered in white silk and set for eight. His eyes settled on Alythia and he stood.

"How'd it go last night?" He slipped a hand into the back pocket of his denim shorts and looked as though he was trying to predict her reply.

Aly didn't make him guess. "Not well." She trailed her fingers along the table's edge. "How's Dane?" He didn't respond and she didn't need him to. Judging from his sour look, it was clear to see that Dane Spears hadn't received a reassuring hug.

"Wonder if anyone else will even bother to show up to this thing?" She hissed an inaudible curse. "Why did Orchid have to get us all tangled up in this mess?"

"I'm kinda glad she did." His tone was soft, matter-of-fact. "We both work too hard to have met any other way."

Aly strolled the patio, seeking to draw calm from the blue sky above that was dotted with puffs of white. "I'm pretty sure the *fun* you and your boys are having on this trip is a far cry from what you're used to."

"You don't want to know what we're used to, Alythia."

"Why so glum?" She mimicked his stance, shoving a hand into a back pocket on her black denim shorts. "Sounds like you've all got successful love lives."

"Sex lives, Alythia. Major difference."

"You're right. A lot less headache."

"Don't be so sure."

"There's no reward in anything more."

"You're wrong. There's the truest reward."

"What do you want from me, Gage?"

Jayson and Orchid arrived before more words could be exchanged. Orchid appeared in high spirits, rushing over to Alythia and tugging her into a fierce hug.

"We need to get out and *do* something, Aly," Orchid was saying as she led her friend away from the men. "Maybe sightseeing or shopping, stopping off for a drink…"

"Orchid?" Aly dragged her feet. "Didn't you hear about last night? With Myrna and Dane?"

"That airhead." Orchid waved her hand. "Just what she asked for.…"

"Orchid! That's a little harsh, isn't it?"

"It is what it is."

"So why is it so important for us to stick around when we aren't getting along?" she asked, hoping the woman would confide in her.

Orchid's smile possessed coyness. "Oh, we got along pretty well to start." She gave Aly a look. "Most of us, anyway." She shrugged, unmindful of her sundress straps easing down her arms. "Jay and I are very close to our friends. We need you guys here—marriage is a serious thing." She rubbed her arms then, briskly, and eased the sundress straps back in place.

"We need our friends around us, Aly, and if everyone's getting along, even better."

"And if we can't get along?"

"Well…" Orchid reached out to tug the hem of Aly's striped Henley tee. "As long as my most levelheaded friend isn't makin' an ass of herself, it's all good."

"Thanks."

Orchid reciprocated Alythia's playful smirk and turned to observe the men talking across the patio. "What I want to know is what's taking you so long to seal the deal with Gage? I want to know if he's as damn good as he looks."

Aly gasped and then dissolved into a wave of laughter. Not long after Alythia burst into a fit of giggles, Orchid followed suit.

"How do you know I haven't 'sealed the deal'?" Aly asked once they had calmed somewhat.

"Sex changes things." Orchid looked across her shoulder again. "He still looks at you like he wants to devour you. He's so intense. The intense ones are usually the freakiest." She turned in time to witness Alythia's reaction and laughed.

Equally amused, Aly took her by the arm and led her to the buffet spread on the patio. "Lack of food has you light-headed. Let's eat."

* * *

Breakfast was a hearty affair and the food disappeared much too quickly, especially once Dane and Zeke arrived. Jeena and Myrna had not graced the group with their presence. Still, Alythia and Orchid used the occasion to make plans for the rest of the trip—time with just the girls. The guys were rolling with laughter over something at their end of the table when one of the two missing guests made an appearance.

"Jeena!" Alythia stood to welcome the woman to the table.

Despite her plans to hop the resort's clubs with her friends, Orchid offered the barest hint of a smile when Jeena approached. Jeena continued her trek toward the end of the table where the men sat talking and laughing over the remains of their breakfast.

Alythia read Jeena's intentions a split second or more before they were put into action. Later she would wonder if she'd withheld her warning out of surprise or spite.

"What the—" Dane's outburst collided with the thunk Jeena's fist made when she landed her blow to the center of Zeke's nape.

The punch sent Zeke face-first into an unfinished bowl of oatmeal. The cereal enhanced by cinnamon and honey had grown cool and had adopted a gummy texture. What remained of the oatmeal was either forced from the sides of the bowl to make way for Zeke's face or it clung to the man's skin, as was evident when he regained control of his faculties and sat upright.

Fearless, Jeena bent to speak directly into one of Zeke's oat-spattered ears. "Think about this the next time you insult somebody, you jackass." She slapped the back of Zeke's head, grinning while she turned away.

Pandemonium erupted before Jeena had even taken a few steps. Orchid, who hadn't given her girlfriend a second's interest, was the first to jump in front of her.

"Dammit, Jeen, what the hell!" Orchid raged, sending Jeena back a few steps with the quick tap she applied to her shoulder. "If you got such a problem with people telling the truth about what you do for a living, then maybe you should stop doing it!"

"Go to hell, Ork! It's not me who's got trouble with truth!" Jeena moved closer to speak in a voice heard by only her, Orchid and Alythia. "Does your soon-to-be hubby know who you came running to for cash after Daddy cut you off? Now are we still in the mood to discuss the truth about how you earned that loan money, Ork?"

"Why are we still friends?" Orchid sneered.

Jeena was equally livid. "That's a question I ask myself daily."

"Well, maybe we shouldn't trouble ourselves with the question anymore."

"Fine by me!"

"Guys—" Alythia tried to make a stab at maintaining order but it was hopeless.

Any attempts at peacemaking could scarcely be heard once Zeke recovered and felt up to defending the blow to his ego. He barreled away from the table, intent on going after Jeena. It took the combined efforts of his friends to turn him from that course of action.

"Let him go!" Jeena refused to retreat and beckoned Zeke forward. "Let the bum-coward go!"

Zeke howled his rage, threatening to break the hold

his friends had on his arms and midriff. Through the melee, Gage and Alythia found each other's eyes. They shook their heads in regret and then focused on separating their friends.

Jeena was bolting through the restaurant with Alythia at her heels. "I don't want to hear it, Aly! Not this time. I'm takin' the first flight the hell out of here."

"I'd ask you to book me a ticket, too, if I didn't have this last meeting with Clive."

Jeena's steps slowed. She smiled and turned back to Aly. "Least one of us got somethin' out of this trip."

"Honey, don't worry about Ork." Alythia gave Jeena's upper arms a squeeze. "She's got a lot on her mind with the wedding and all."

"Aly girl, I don't plan on worrying about Orchid Benjamin ever again. I've had enough of this freak show we call a friendship." Jeena made a show of wiping her hands and then gave Aly's cheek a soft pat. "When you start being honest with yourself, you'll realize you've had enough, too."

"We've been through worse."

"Hmph." Jeena leaned her head back and inhaled deeply. "You know our band of misfits would've busted up a long time ago if it hadn't been for you always being the peacemaker."

Aly hugged herself. "I'm no peacemaker."

"You are, and so much so that I bet you haven't even gotten to have much fun with Gage because of all this mess."

"I didn't come here for that."

"Oh, come off it, girl. I've seen him, remember?"

Aly gave a teasing smile. "I don't think he's so impressed with me. I wasn't even inducted into the mile-high club."

"Consider yourself lucky. Look at where membership got the rest of us."

Aly's playful smile began to wane. "Mur says he's a playa—the 'hit 'em and quit 'em' kind."

"And it's most likely true," Jeena solemnly conceded. "What man wouldn't use a face and body like he has to enjoy women and often? But I doubt Mur was looking out for you when she said it. She's just upset because she never had the chance to go after him herself."

"And what about you?" Aly smoothed a tuft of Jeena's clipped hair behind her ear. "You were going after him, too, wanted him to become a client."

"No, Aly, not that, never that!" Jeena laughed. "I want space in that new high-rise of his." Her amusement doused suddenly. "It's gonna be next to impossible getting him to take me seriously now, with him thinking I'd be running a brothel out of it."

Aly led Jeena to a less trafficked area of the lobby. "So what *are* your plans for it?"

"A career placement office." Jeena looked to Aly as though expecting her to laugh and nodded appreciatively when she didn't. "I, um…I want to get some of my…escorts out of the business. So many of them wind up doing certain things out of sheer desperation and what they perceive as failure in the real world. A place like this could help." She nodded then, more deliberately. "They wouldn't feel self-conscious that the folks in my office would be looking down on them for *any* reason."

"It's a great idea, Jeen." Aly squeezed her arm.

"Yeah…it would've been, but I can forget it now that

Gage's good buddy is probably back there putting the last nail in my coffin."

"Well, don't forget…you, um, probably had just a teeny bit to do with that. Don't give up, okay?" Alythia urged once they'd stopped laughing.

"I won't…." Jeena considered, working kinks out of her neck. "Gage isn't the only one who makes the decisions anyway. There's a long list of stuffed shirts that get to chime in and choose the best bid."

"Bid?" Aly's bright eyes narrowed. "For renting office space?"

"Not just any office space. *Prime* real estate in the heart of downtown."

"You're sure?" Aly felt her breath grow labored. "Sure it belongs to Gage?"

"No, and that's the thing. He's keeping his name out of the forefront."

"Then how do you—"

"I come across a lot of info in my line of work. Gage Vincent may make all his money being the *top* dog, but he doesn't make it by being the *only* dog. He's very good at placing people right where he wants them."

"But you're sure he's the lead in all this?"

"Well, nothing's for sure." Jeena leaned against the wall. "Unfortunately, none of my clients are members of his inner circle regarding the thing, so I decided to take a stab at talking to Gage directly." She studied her manicure and shrugged. "Once Orchid and Jay announced their engagement, I figured…one mutual friend looking out for another mutual friend and all that jazz…."

"Right…" Aly dropped down onto the arm of a nearby chair, her thoughts on the building she herself was hoping to secure lodgings inside.

"Right." Jeena's smile was sour yet easy. "I'm gonna go and book that flight." She tugged Aly into a hug. "Thanks, sweetie."

Alythia watched Jeena until she had disappeared into a small crowd gathered in the elevator bay.

"Margarita sampler, ma'am?"

Alythia tuned in to a smiling young woman who was garbed in a metallic blue bikini with a stark white wrap tied asymmetrically over the bottom. On her palms, she balanced a round tray of margarita shots.

Aly took one of the shots and downed it. "Forget the samples and lead me to the nearest pitcher," she said.

Aly's midmorning meeting with Clive Weeks was two parts laughter and light chatter and one part business. She'd all but camped out at the seaside bar that the helpful waitress with the tray of margaritas had guided her to. When she'd asked Clive if he would mind moving the meeting there, he'd been all too pleased by the location change.

Another pitcher of margaritas later, the two had shaken hands on the deal. Clive had even spoken to his lawyer about the preliminary paperwork to set things in motion. When Clive and Aly had parted ways, she maintained her comfy spot on the cushiony peach sofa that occupied one corner of the terrace. After several long moments of people and view watching, she called Marianne to share news of the Anegada boutique and then breached the subject she'd really called to discuss.

"Well, info about who the decision makers are is being closely guarded but..." Marianne's sigh came over her end of the line "...rumor is that Vincent is the 'top dog' just like Jeena said."

"Rumor? Do you think that's all it is?"

"So far? Well, yeah…but a person wouldn't have to do much homework to put something like that together. It's no secret that he's leasing several office spaces in that building. It stands to reason that he'd go about acquiring the rest and just own the building outright. Everybody knows the man is as smart as he is patient. It's one of the things that makes him so successful."

Aly felt a sharp chill and began to curse the shorts she'd donned that morning. "Is there any way to make sure, Mari?"

"Well, there's always a way. I've heard some of our competitors for the new space have already…reached out, sending bribes to some of the top folks."

"Money?"

"Money, sex, promises for sex." Marianne ticked off the list.

"Great." Aly feathered fingers across her brow.

"You all right, hon?"

Aly smiled and shook her head. "I'm good, but I'd feel a lot better if you could find out who we're really looking to go into business with."

Feeling depleted and defeated following her chat with Marianne, Alythia decided that an escape to the beach was in order. She certainly couldn't get into any trouble there. At least, that was what she hoped when she made her way to a surprisingly quiet strip a ways down from the beachfront bar.

Armed with one of the bar's fruity drinks and a tote bag of top picks from her reading list, Alythia set out for some hopefully uneventful time to herself. Inspired by the margarita-promoting waitress from earlier that day, Aly had slipped into her most daring two-piece for her quiet escape. Still, she kept the lavender bikini hidden beneath a cover-up until she'd reached a more private stretch of beach.

"Hiding?"

"Is it that obvious?" Alythia pulled off her floppy straw hat and looked up at Gage, who stood just a few feet away.

"Just a little." He took a couple of small steps closer to her, shuffling the fine sand beneath his black sandals as he moved. "Not a very good spot, you know?"

She smiled, staring out over the serene and utterly striking blue waters. "I really didn't expect it to be completely foolproof."

A teasing wince narrowed his liquid brown stare. "Ouch."

Alythia winced, as well. "Gage—"

"Would you come with me?"

"I— Come…where?"

"A better hiding place."

Alythia gave a little shrug, following Gage's eyes faltering to the valley between her breasts, which were emphasized by the cut of her bikini top. "This one looks pretty good to me."

"You'll disagree with that soon enough."

"You sound sure of that." She visored a hand to her brow to study him more accurately.

"I've got every reason to."

"So? Where is this oasis?" When he simply looked toward the water, Alythia frowned his way for a second before she followed the direction of his gaze. She hadn't noticed the sailboat before and wondered if he had orchestrated the navigation to coincide with his response.

"A jet and a boat, Mr. Vincent. I'm impressed." Aly appeared anything but as she returned her attention to the book she'd been reading.

"I'll keep that in mind when I buy a sailboat." He nodded toward the sea. "That one belongs to Clive." He circled her slowly, retrieving her cover-up from where she'd tossed it over her tote bag. "Come with me. You'll be able to read a lot more out there than over here."

"Oh?" She closed her book. "Because we'll be all alone out there and uninterrupted?"

"There's that." He smiled, sparking the deep single dimple as he rubbed her cover-up between his fingers. "Aside from the crew, we'll be on our own but I was referring to the sun." He squinted toward the gorgeous skies above. "You wouldn't want to risk damaging that skin." His expression was blatantly appraising as his eyes trailed her body.

Alythia couldn't deny his point. She had brought a folding seat but hadn't thought to bring an umbrella. Gage then offered his hand. Aly regarded him only a few more seconds before she accepted his hospitality. Gathering her belongings, she stood. Gage relieved her of her things, helped her into her cover-up and escorted her in the direction of the pier.

"Incredible." Despite her hesitation, Aly couldn't fake nonchalance and act as though the view from the bow of the boat wasn't extraordinary.

"Thanks," she said in reference to both the refill on her mojito and the hour of solitude she'd enjoyed aboard the boat.

Gage gave her a mock toast with his own glass. "Thanks for coming along." He sipped of his mojito and then turned his back on the view to study her instead. "I wasn't sure where we stood after this morning."

"Do you mind if we don't…?" Aly set down her drink and returned to the two lounge chairs covered by a massive umbrella.

"Not a problem." Gage swallowed back half of his mojito and joined Aly.

"Clive's really created something special here, hasn't he?" Aly drew her legs up to her chest and regarded the expanse of blue sea and sky as far as she could see.

"Yeah…he's, um…he's got a habit of spotting that kind of thing."

Alythia looked over her shoulder, intending to ply Gage with an agreeable look. The raw hunger she saw in his eyes froze her instead. When he moved to close the distance between them, she shook her head.

"Gage—" Surprise had rendered her speechless, incapable of finishing her statement. He'd taken her by the waist and placed her in a straddle across his lap, relieving her of her cover-up as he did. He settled her beautifully and Aly could feel herself melting when he was nudging the middle of her bikini bottom with the obvious erection beneath his denim shorts. He fondled one cheek while his other hand disappeared into her hair, drawing her into his kiss.

Aly could hear herself moaning even before their tongues engaged. Her nails rasped across the silken whiskers darkening his gorgeous face as her full lips suckled his tongue. She withdrew from the kiss, biting her lip on a moan when his thumb drifted to her thighs and he began a stunning assault on the nub of sheer sensation above her femininity. She shuddered, overwhelmed by wave after wave of delight as he worked the nub with greater intensity.

He laid her across the two chairs, slowly relieving her of the bikini top with long tugs of the ties that secured the garment. She was barely halfway out of the top when his face was buried between the pert, dewy globes.

For a time, he nuzzled his face in her cleavage, sighing her name as he did so. Alythia arched sharply when he helped himself to a ravenous suckling of her firming nipples. Then, incredibly, she was being treated to another marvelous caress when his fingers grazed the petals of her womanhood. Just barely did he venture inside her walls. Alythia hungered for him. She desperately circled her hips on his slight caress.

"Gage…"

She could say nothing further, but apparently the sigh of his name was enough to cool Gage's hormones.

"You're right," he said, pressing a last kiss to the valley between her heaving breasts. Withdrawing his fingers, he drew her top back into place and smiled down. "This isn't the place."

"No." She shook her head. "No, Gage, I didn't mean—"

He silenced her with a soft kiss. "We should head back anyway. The crew is discreet but we shouldn't push it."

"Gage?" She pushed herself up on the lounge when he left her.

Chapter 9

As flavorful tropical drinks with charming umbrellas had kept Aly in a calm frame of mind for much of the day, she figured, why tinker with what was working? She took a late lunch in her suite, refusing to acknowledge the voice that cried "coward" in her mind.

She'd told Clive that she'd be leaving early and the man insisted on treating her to dinner before she vanished. A phone call to Jeena proved to be the bright spot when the woman shared that she wouldn't be leaving until 11:00 a.m. the next day.

Alythia talked her friend into getting dolled up and meeting for drinks before her dinner with Clive. Jeena was in so long as drinks were involved. Aly was glad Jeena hadn't asked why she wasn't trying to spend the evening with Gage. Though Aly still needed confirmation on whether Gage was connected to that building.

But didn't she have that already? And why did it matter? She hadn't done anything wrong. It wasn't as if she'd been trying to seduce him into accepting her bid.

No. She *hadn't* been, but she hadn't had all the facts, either. What would it mean for her to have them and not tell him? Especially if their relationship became more…physical? She wished herself luck with that and refused to think of what had happened between them earlier on the boat. Besides, if the man was as smart as he seemed, then he'd simply write her off as another wild woman, given what he'd seen over the two and a half days they'd known each other.

Then was not the time to think of that, though, Aly decided. Not with another fruity drink calling her name. Still, she checked the clockface visible beneath the bracelets adorning her wrists.

"We hear you're leaving us, miss," a bartender noted when Alythia had claimed a spot at the L-shaped glass bar in the restaurant where she was to meet Clive.

"Word travels fast." Aly didn't hide the surprise from her face.

"Friends of Mr. Weeks's get our highest attention, of course."

"Of course." Aly smiled.

"On the house." The man presented a glass of wine.

Smile widening, Aly raised the glass in toast. "Thank you." She sipped, relishing the cool and subtly fruity taste of the blend against her tongue before she swallowed. She turned on the stool and observed the area and was energized by all the bodies moving to the affecting rhythms produced by the band that had come in from St. Croix to perform that evening. She had tried to encourage Jeena to stay a while longer and enjoy more of the band, perhaps do a little dancing, but Jeena was obviously in no mood to try her luck with another member of the opposite sex. Alythia celebrated her friend's decision, her smile waning when Dane Spears came into her line of sight.

"Don't go, please." Dane raised his hands, seeing Alythia preparing to scoot from the barstool. "I just want to apologize."

"You don't owe one. Not to me."

Dane's lips thinned as he accepted her meaning. "I'm still sorry that things got so out of hand." He shrugged, sending a quick ripple through the snug crimson crew shirt he wore. "Once it all started to go off track, nobody knew how to get it right again."

"Dane—" Aly sighed impatiently and then deigned to give him a quick glare "—just because we have mutual friends about to marry doesn't mean we're obligated to be friends." Again she made a move to leave.

"Please." Dane moved before her. "I really do feel bad about all this." He dropped a hand to her shoulder, left bare by the flirty swing dress she sported.

Aly gave a pointed look toward his hand, which he promptly removed. "It's in the past." She slipped off the barstool, leaving him no choice but to back away. "The resort's a big place with more people coming in every day. I'm sure we'll all make new friends soon enough."

Dane nodded, his gaze appraising. "I see why G's so attached to you."

Alythia smiled, resisting the urge to roll her eyes.

Dane moved closer. "Things might've been nicer had I met you first."

"Ahh…Dane…I don't know." Her smile becoming more genuine, Alythia retrieved her drink from the bar.

"Slapping and punching necks really isn't my speed. I like to aim for places a bit more memorable." With that said, she threw a sultrier element into her stare and let her gaze drift below Dane's waist. She waited until his expression confirmed that she was understood and then left him standing alone at the bar.

Despite Alythia's underlying threat, Dane had apparently not taken full benefit of the hint. He looked ready to follow but instead ventured in the opposite direction.

Gage was relieved to see Dane walking away from the bar area, since his friends were the last people he wanted to see. He was too busy hoping his scheme with Clive, albeit contrived, would work. He'd played a hunch that Alythia would want to catch the first flight back to Charlotte following another disastrous exchange between their friends.

Once Clive had confirmed that, the two put their heads together and had come up with the goodbye dinner to celebrate the beginning of their new business alliance. What Alythia didn't know was that Gage would be her dinner partner instead of Clive. Gage could only hope that evening would fare better than all the rest.

When he arrived at the restaurant and set eyes on his intended date, Gage could only chuckle over his new stream of rotten luck. Alythia had taken a place on one of the four long rust-colored sofas that had been situated to form cozy seating in the clearing that separated the restaurant's bar and dining areas.

Of course, the area being located in virtually the middle of the place made it impossible to miss anyone seated there—especially any *woman* seated there alone and most especially when she looked like Alythia Duffy.

Apparently the man cozied up next to her had decided to stake a claim instead of merely observing.

"Having your usual, Mr. V?" a bartender inquired when Gage propped an elbow on one of the high-backed chairs. The man was already placing Gage's favorite brew on the counter.

"How long's Miss Duffy been here?" Gage asked, still watching Alythia across the room.

"About fifteen minutes, sir. She was talking with Mr. Spears a little earlier."

"Hell," Gage grumbled too low for the barkeep to hear. "Is he still around?"

"I saw him not long ago. I'm sure I can track him down for you, sir."

"Don't bother." Gage threw back a swig of the beer, dropped several bills to the bar and stood.

Alythia laughed over conversation from the man seated a bit too close to her. That laughter curbed when she saw him straighten and appear less amused as he stared up over her head. She turned, following the line of the man's gaze, looking back and up.

"Gage?" She didn't mask her surprise at finding him next to the sofa. "What—"

"Clive asked me to join you guys for dinner."

"Oh…" She blinked and then waved toward the man seated at her right. "Roger Harrison, Gage Vincent." She waited for the men to shake hands. Her eyes widened a fraction when she noticed Roger wincing when Gage squeezed his hand.

"Nice to meet you." Gage coolly released his hold

on Roger's hand to take Alythia's arm and guide her up from the sofa.

"Uh, Roger, it—it's nice talking to you," Aly threw over her shoulder while she was unceremoniously escorted away.

"We're leaving?" she queried, noticing the restaurant exit in their path. She received no answer and wasn't too surprised. Aly waited until they'd taken an elevator and had ascended a few floors before she fixed Gage with a smug, narrowed look.

"Tsk, tsk, Mr. Vincent. Using business to secure your pleasure. Not very professional," she gibed, studying the twinkle of lights on the panel while the car traveled up.

The words had only just passed her lips when he came to stand before her and blocked everything from her sight.

"Neither is this," he said and filled her mouth with his tongue moments later.

Alythia lost the power to command her legs and simply rested back on the paneled siding of the car. She took Gage with her, curving her fingers lightly about the collar of his shirt, wanting him close while she swayed.

Gage braced a hand on the wall to steady himself, while the other maintained a firm grasp about her neck. His thumb positioned beneath her chin, keeping it propped and perfectly aligned to receive his tongue, which outlined, filled and stroked her mouth. Deft, exploring lunges forced telling moans from her throat.

Aly moaned anew at the sound of the elevator dinging to announce their arrival. The moan was one of disappointment. It gained volume when Gage broke the kiss to rain more along her neck and collarbone.

"Stay…" she begged him, raking her nails through

the sleek cap of dark brown crowning his head and on to the silky whiskers beginning to roughen his strong jaw. She didn't want to leave the confines of the car, truly fearing their moment would end.

Gage returned no reply. Instead, he kissed his way down her frame. In the process, he hit a button on the elevator's control panel, prolonging their exit.

"Gage…" She swallowed, biting her lip and giving in to the strong waves of arousal as he went to his knees before her. "Cameras in the elevator—"

"Not this one," he said, interrupting her gasp.

Powerfully crafted hands roamed her long legs, beautifully shaped and accentuated by a pair of dazzling glasslike sandals. His touch journeyed upward and back toward her thighs in the wake of his mouth. Anticipation ruled Alythia's actions and within seconds she felt a warm rush of moisture collecting on her palms.

Gage's head had disappeared beneath a swath of dress material. The sight of him there sent quivers through her body, forcing her flush into overdrive. Aly felt him there at the crotch of her panties and bit down hard on her bottom lip when she heard his grunt. His nose was nudging the fragrant moistness clinging to her lingerie.

"Gage, I—I'm—" She heard his muffled chuckle and knew he'd correctly guessed that she was about to apologize for her loss of control.

"Will you say you're sorry every time you come apart on me?" Though muffled, his words resonated on the commanding chords of his rich voice.

Alythia couldn't answer and he didn't press, preferring to take her reaction to what he subjected her to as a response. Using the tip of his talented tongue, he traced the stitching along the crotch of her underwear. All the while, he inhaled deeply of her natural fragrance. Aly maintained a desperate hold on his shoulders. The crisp black shirt he wore did nothing to mask their breadth or power. Her fingers flexed into the fabric, fortifying her grip until her hands lost the ability to grasp anything.

Soon her fingers were splayed out along either side of her against the car's paneling. She shouldn't have been concerned about losing her balance. Gage had her secure in his palms, cradling her ample bottom as he intensified his exploration of her body. One hand slipped, gliding around her thigh to allow his thumb a more intimate sampling.

Alythia's lips formed a dual bow when they parted in relish over the touch. She pressed her head against the wall, moving it back and forth out of sheer enjoyment of the curious thumb stroking her femininity outlined against the silky fabric of her lingerie. Then the digit was venturing inside, stroking the slick flesh without the barrier of material.

"Gage—" She'd hoped to choke out more than his name, needing to explain that she was then wholly incapable of controlling her body's reactions. The explanation died on her tongue when his seeking thumb rotated just inside her puckered entrance and then eased in farther.

Gage rose to his full height, keeping his hand and stroking thumb in place. He watched Alythia taking what he gave her, loving the small helpless sounds she shared each time he deepened the stroke or changed its direction. His hypnotic liquid stare never leaving her face, he hit another button on the car's control panel.

Only then did he deprive Aly of his touch to swing her up into his arms.

There were no other guests in sight as they exited the elevator car and arrived in a bedroom.

"Oh." She gave a mild start, blinking in wonder at her surroundings. "My room doesn't do this…." Her voice was small as she studied her surroundings.

"Only two of them do," he explained, carrying her deeper into the room. "The other belongs to Clive in his apartment."

"Clive's very nice to his friends."

"Yeah, he's a peach." Gage reengaged the kiss as the last word silenced on his tongue. He continued a deep exploration of her mouth.

Alythia kissed Gage with an unmasked hunger that gave him the impression that she had no interest in spending their time talking. With a flex of her toes, she angled her foot to maneuver out of the strapless sandals. She arched into his chest when her shoes hit the floor. A smile curved her lips. In moments, Gage swiftly turned Aly so that her back now cushioned the bed that seemed to occupy the entire side of the room.

Their disrobing was frenzied. One quick tug at the row of fastenings below her arm took Aly from her dress to leave her clothed in the sheer panties he had kissed his way through moments earlier. He pulled her hands away when she would have helped him from his clothes. Pressing her wrists to the bed, he gave them a warning press to instruct her to leave them there.

Then he was settling back on his haunches, taking his time to observe her, study her covered by only the scrap of panties. He looked as though he couldn't decide which part of her he wanted to help himself to first.

Again Aly bit down on her lip. Tentatively, she moved to stroke his thigh, hidden but no less potent beneath the dark material of his trousers. She smiled when he permitted the action. Gage took her hand then, lifting it, turning it over to tongue her palm. Aly used her free hand to tug at the tail of his shirt, already conveniently outside his trousers.

Then she was the one taking inventory of what he bared to her view. Aly reached out, intending to stroke his rigid pack but became distracted by the pronounced ridge beneath his zipper.

Wonder filling her eyes, she applied the lightest strokes to the bulge. He let his head slope forward and she grew bolder with her touch. Gage let himself be pleasured for only a moment. He'd wanted her since he'd seen her and having her there threatened to dissolve all that was left of his restraint. He squeezed her hand and left the bed.

Alythia watched him finish disrobing. Her amethyst stare followed every garment that fell, greedily absorbing all that was revealed. She was moving to slip out of her panties when he returned to the bed. Once again Gage caught her hand. He wanted to handle that part himself and did so with relish.

Her quivering returned when he covered her body with his. Immediately, Aly began to luxuriate in the feel of his rich café noir skin creating the most delicious friction against the milky caramel of hers. Still, she moved beneath him with a subtle urgency. Gage resumed raining his famished kisses along her collarbone and then he was cradling her plump, pert breasts for suckling.

Alythia's subtle moves grew even more urgent, renewed moisture pooling in her panties. The incessant nibbling at her firming nipples threw her hormones into a state of frenzy. His perfect teeth subjected the buds to a sensual bruising, his tongue easing in to supply a soothing bath and his wonderfully crafted lips participating in the erotic performance sent Aly gasping and bucking her hips wildly against his.

Gage abandoned the task, his molten chocolate gaze narrowing while an arrogant smirk curved his mouth in response to the state he saw he was leaving her in. He moved lower in the wide bed, giving enthusiastic attention to her belly button until she wriggled uncontrollably and emitted a tiny shriek amid her gasps and moans. He eased the panties down from her hips, dousing each patch of newly exposed skin with a brush from his lips. Once the lacy garment was completely discarded, he settled himself, resting his head on the base of her belly and inhaling as though her scent held some fortifying capability.

Aly raked her nails across the close-cut hair covering his head, feeling him nudge her hand when he moved to outline the Brazilian-waxed triangle above her treasure. Her body arched into a perfect bow when his nose nudged her clit. She trembled wickedly when his lips followed. Gage feasted on her until her hips made a tangle of the turned-down sheets.

Alythia settled into a pool of emotion when his tongue claimed her. The first stroke was deep and branding and she could hear herself panting. The intimate kiss was tireless, robust and provocatively infectious. Gage kept her bottom cradled in his wide palms, lifting her inescapably into the act. His groan carried a ravenous quality as he drank deeply of her.

Soon Alythia could hear sounds of pleading coming from her throat. She wanted all of him and her patience had worn itself out.

Alythia felt a telltale nudging against her pubic bone and she opened her eyes to find Gage setting protection in place. Her hand brushed his in an attempt to offer assistance. The gesture was more erotic than assisting. He shuddered once, incapable of doing more. He rained a long lazy kiss across her clavicle and left Alythia to guide him inside her.

She handled the task with great interest and fabulous delight. The feel of him filling her hand was a treat in itself. She wanted to keep him there almost as much as she wanted him inside her.

That was before she got him inside her. They groaned in sync and seemed to melt deeper into the bed when they were one. Gage wrested out the most helpless sounds that had Aly savoring twin emotions of empowerment and desire. Her triumph over shattering him so was only curbed by his command over her body. His hold was unbreakable at her hips as he filled her, stretched her, rotated and retreated only to replay the move with unfailing eagerness.

Alythia was desperate to wrap her legs about his waist and take him until she passed out from exhaustion and satisfaction. She accepted that she'd have to settle for accomplishing that without the aid of encircling his lean hips between her thighs. Gage kept his hands on her upper thighs, rendering her immobile while he pleasured her as well as himself. His lunges were slow, yet his ability to keep them that way warred with the desire for total surrender inside her.

That desire won and Aly felt her breathing hitch

when he spent himself inside the condom, which was thin enough for her to feel the steady pulse of his release. The sensation made her convulse with pleasure, she was so elated by the rapture threading its way through her. Then she was the one who shattered, giving herself over to the thrill.

Chapter 10

Alythia woke feeling excited and hopeful for the first time since setting out on the grand escape with her friends. She let her eyes drift shut again and snuggled back into Gage. She'd forgotten how many rounds of lovemaking there had been the night before. Afterward he'd drawn her back into him, spooning her into the unrelenting length of muscle and bone that was his body.

Aly had fallen asleep almost instantly. She willed herself back to sleep then, not wanting the day to begin just yet. How she wished the pressures of the day could wait before they intervened. How she hoped to stave off certain revelations, thinking of the confirmation Marianne was sure to have of a certain Charlotte, NC, skyscraper belonging to the man who kept her a willing captive in his arms then.

Aly wiggled against Gage, hoping to at least wake

him. He was dead to the world. Just as well, she thought, hearing the distinctive chimes of her mobile singing a high-pitched melody throughout the rooms of the suite.

Marianne, Aly thought, deciding to let the call go to voice mail. She'd have her answers soon enough. For now, she'd savor a little more time with this man and the dreamscape they'd created together.

Alythia raised her head from the pillow when her phone chimed again. Dread crept through her in response to the sound that time. Moaning softly, she set her head back on the pillow. That wasn't Marianne. This call was coming from a much closer distance and voice mail was most likely not an option.

Besides, she didn't want to risk waking Gage. If this was another act in the great friendship melodrama, then he would hear about it soon enough.

With that, she carefully pulled back the covers that had sheltered their bodies from the cool sea air that had billowed past the wispy curtains during the night. She slipped into the shirt Gage had discarded the night before and made it across the expansive bedroom in time to dig the phone out of the purse she had dropped the night before. She answered just as the third installment of rings began.

"What?"

"Aly, thank God!" Jeena's hysterical voice met the whispered greeting.

"Jeen, not now. I had a really, *really* good night and I was hoping to at least carry it over until lunchtime. Now, unless you're calling me because you need a ride to the air—"

"I decided to take a later flight out."

"Why?" Aly rolled her eyes when she blurted the

query, but she knew the damage was done: her curiosity would not rest until it was sated. "What happened?"

"It's not good."

The reply sent Aly to the arm of the chair she stood closest to. Disbelief stowed away inside her with every syllable she listened to Jeena utter. Later, Aly shut off the phone, holding it to her chest while she bowed her head. She realized she was holding her breath and ordered herself to inhale several times. A small measure of calm was beginning to settle in when she was plucked off the chair.

Gage had gathered her up against him. Kissing her neck, he carried her back to bed, unmindful of her soft urgings for him to wait. He wouldn't and continued his journey. He held her before him and trailed his nose from her collarbone to the sensitive spot behind her ear. His urgency to resume what they'd spent the better part of the evening doing was contagious.

Alythia didn't take much persuading. She let Gage have his way, all the while praying that he'd have his way vigorously. Their interlude was brief but no less sweet than all the others had been.

Gage tumbled her into the bed, only managing to take Alythia halfway out of his shirt, as he was more preoccupied with putting on protection in order to take what he wanted from her. Laughter flooded the room, what with all the kissing amid disrobing and condom applying. He wasn't inside her long before he was coming hard, his touch so overtly possessive that she was following suit moments later. She reveled in the feel of sensuality and freedom she found in his arms.

Afterward, they lay embracing and then Aly treated

her fingers to one final drift across the fabulous carving of his abs and perfect chest.

"I really need to go," she moaned.

"I want to see you later. Here." He murmured the words, eyes closed while he played with her hair.

Alythia didn't answer, instead making a move from the bed. Gage's relaxed pose was merely a veil for the reflexes that launched into action when he felt her attempting to leave him. He put her on her back, securing her to the bed as he covered her.

His features sharpened as his observation of her gained depth. "What is it?"

"Gage—"

"Something's off with you. What?"

She closed her eyes, mentally thumbing through a list of appropriate excuses. "Just some work stuff I need to talk to Clive about since I, um, didn't have the chance to last night." Gage's phone rang then and she valiantly hid her relief. "Is that you?" she asked him.

"It can wait." Gage never looked in the direction of the ring. "It's not just Clive. What else, Alythia?"

"Gage." She pushed herself up and worked to set him off kilter with a sudden and thorough kiss when he would have put her on her back again.

"I really need to go." She spoke the words into his mouth, scratching his rough cheek before breaking the kiss.

Gage reclined against the cushioning that ran the extensive length of the bed's headboard. He watched as she gathered her things from where they had fallen during their heated undressing the night before.

"Should I come and get you later?" He folded his arms over his bare chest. His voice had gone softer, harboring a knowing intensity as though he expected a runaround on the answer.

Alythia's resulting smile held the same knowing intensity. "I'm guessing that later you'll have your hands pretty full."

His phone rang again as if to confirm her suspicion.

"You should get that." She found the bathroom, changed quickly and left him soon after.

"Where is she?"

"Trying to sleep." Jeena's voice sounded as weary as Alythia felt. She took a seat on a swivel chair in the living area of Orchid's suite. "What the hell happened, Jeen?" The details of the earlier phone conversation were still wreaking confusing havoc in her mind.

Jeena groaned, scrubbing her bare face in her palms. "Apparently, the bad vibes finally rolled around to the bride and groom."

"But how?" Alythia spread her hands when she braced her elbows against the turquoise capris she'd changed into after leaving Gage's suite and grabbing a shower in her own room.

"They argued again about all this...damn drama." Jeena reclined in an awkward spread-eagle position on the chair opposite Alythia. "Jayson said he'd considered how long it'd be before she started acting like her friends...blah, blah, blah...."

"So she goes and proves him right?" Aly sounded incredulous, shaking her head when Jeena shrugged. "So how'd it balloon into all the rest?"

Jeena was apparently in no more of a mood to discuss "the rest" than she had been when she'd called Alythia earlier. The look on her face proved it, but she seemed to resolve herself to confess it anyway.

"Myrna caused it to balloon."

"Myrna? But I thought Jayson—"

"Myrna went to make up with Dane."

Aly's groan accompanied her eyes closing.

"And the answer to your question is no, the girl will never learn. She wanted to surprise Dane, had the maids open his room door so she could *wake him up*. He was already...up with Orchid."

"Jesus." Aly clenched her fingers in her hair and gave a tug. "Can this get any messier?"

"Please." Jeena raised her hands as if she were trying to ward off any bad vibes Aly might have unknowingly released with her query. "Don't even ask that. Myrna ran screaming to Jayson and now we're here. Orchid's in the bedroom nursing a bruised cheek from her fiancé."

"So what are *you* gonna do next?" Jeena asked Aly once they'd absorbed a few minutes of silence.

"Clearly there's no reason for any of us to stay. Guess you're not the only one on the way to the airport."

"Wait a minute." Jeena straightened in the chair. "You'd go back to Charlotte now? What about Gage?"

"You said it yourself." Aly's voice had taken on progressively more weariness. "The bad vibes finally rolled around to the bride and groom. Won't be long before they roll around to me and Gage."

"I don't believe that, Aly."

"I slept with him." Alythia spread her hands as though nothing more needed to be said. "I slept with him and I've known him all of what? Two days?"

"And the problem? It was consensual, right?"

Alythia felt the genuine urge to laugh. "Consent? Not hard to get from a woman whose friends have all slept with *his* friends. Just the natural order of things, right?" She bowed her head. "I'm sorry, Jeen…."

"Don't be." Jeena scooted to the edge of the chair. "And Gage isn't his friends. I don't believe he's stupid enough to buy that 'you are who you hang with' crap."

"It's usually a pretty good indicator." Aly smiled at herself. "In spite of what you've always thought, I'm no Goody Two-Shoes. It didn't take much persuasion from Gage." She blinked. "I don't think he had to persuade me much at all. We were pretty much on the same page."

"Of course you were!" Jeena blurted, kicking out a bare foot to emphasize her conviction. "*You* are a dime and Gage… A woman would have to be blind and lacking a shred of emotion not to be affected by what he puts out."

"Do you know why I'm always working?" Aly asked once she'd considered Jeena's words for a time. "Finding a man is…difficult when he has certain assumptions."

"Do you really think Gage has those assumptions?"

"No, I really don't." Aly shrugged. "But sooner or later he will. Just look at what happened between Jay and Ork." Faintly, a voice reminded her that particular love match had been orchestrated.

"Have you ever considered giving the man the benefit of the doubt?" Jeena was asking.

"I did." Aly left the chair and began a slow pace of the room. "This trip has me looking at a lot of things I never bothered to consider before, though. That happily-ever-after Myrna's so desperate to find? I want it, too." She leaned against the frame of the glass doors overlooking the ocean view. "I'm not saying I expect to find it with a man like Gage, but that…that would've been nice." *More than nice,* she admitted quietly.

"This thing between Jay and Ork, compounded with what's already gone down… I don't know if we'd stand a chance."

"And you're too much of a wuss to find out," Jeena accused, looking in Aly's direction.

"Hey, hey? Shouldn't you be in bed?" Clive asked when he found Gage reclining in one of the lounges behind *Alythia's* upcoming boutique later that afternoon.

Gage tried to gain some satisfaction from the breeze drifting over his face and beneath the blue cotton T-shirt that hung outside his jeans.

"She's gone," he said.

"Damn." Clive grimaced and then dropped to the lounge next to Gage. "Sorry our plan didn't work to get you guys a little time alone."

"Oh, it worked." Gage grinned self-indulgently. "It worked very well, and thank you very much. Problem is that reality intervened, as it usually does."

"So what happened?"

Gage made quick work of explaining the latest upset. "So instead of a wedding, we may all wind up having seats to a trial. Orchid says she's bringing Jay up on assault charges."

"That *is* a mess." Clive stroked his dimpled chin and then frowned. "What does that have to do with you and Alythia, though?"

"Not a damn thing." Gage's full, robust laughter came through. "But we keep getting caught up in it just the same."

"So you're just gonna hang out here for the rest of the trip?"

"Why not? Already got a great view for it."

"So you're just gonna let it go?"

"Maybe I should, man...." Gage mopped a hand across his face and scratched the smattering of whiskers that threw his face into further shadow. "Everything that's happened... It's been nothin' but a mess."

"And is that what you think of when you think of you and her together? A mess?" Clive received no answer and seemed to take it as a good sign. "Are you gonna let her go?"

"Hell, no, I'm not."

The fierce response spoken abruptly and without hesitation brought a satisfied smile to Clive's face. "So what are you waiting on?"

"I don't know *how* to go after her." Gage shook his head when he heard the hearty laughter coming from Clive's direction. He didn't begrudge the reaction.

"Since when do *you* have confusion about going after the opposite sex?" Clive teased.

"Never wanted to try playing for keeps before." Gage's reply was simply spoken.

Clive sobered. "You really feel that way about her or is it just that you're not ready for her to leave your bed yet?"

"I *never* want her to leave my bed." Gage gave Clive a level gaze. "But that's about sex. I still don't know what else it is about her that I can't shake. The sex was..." He closed his eyes, obviously working to locate the proper descriptive word or phrase.

Clive smirked, wind whipping light hair about his tanned face. "I got it."

"But there's more and I—I mean it when I say I don't know *how* to go after her."

"Well maybe it's not something you can plot or strategize over like a business deal." Clive stood. "Maybe it's one of those things you're just gonna have to trust your gut on."

"Hell, Clive—" Gage worked the heels of his hands into his eyes "—that's what got us all into this mess."

"Sounds like you need to decide whether you're gonna sit here until the perfect plan materializes before the woman you want distances herself physically *and* emotionally." Clive dropped a playful slap to Gage's cheek, then his shoulder and then turned to leave.

Gage studied the vibrant view with bland interest for a time before he dug out his mobile.

"All is well, boss," Webb confirmed when he answered after two rings.

"Glad to hear it." Gage settled down deeper on the lounge, holding the phone at his ear using the crook of his shoulder. "That's not why I'm calling. I need you to help me find someone."

Chapter 11

Alythia decided to focus on work. It was the one thing that she hadn't screwed up. She had decided not to return to North Carolina with everyone else. Despite their misunderstandings, Jeena and Orchid went back to Charlotte together, Orchid on the warpath with Jayson Muns in her sight. Myrna had suddenly discovered she had a photo shoot that had taken her off to parts unknown. Word was that the guys had all returned together.

Aly could only imagine how heated *that* onboard conversation had become. No, she was in no hurry to return home. Instead, she decided to pay another visit to Aspen and her boutique there. There was nothing that required her immediate attention, other than inventory, which her staff could handle as well as or better than she could.

Nevertheless, Alythia needed the escape. As cowardly as the move might have been, she needed the time to herself. She needed the stillness, the peace of mind the place provided.

That peace was one of her main reasons for selecting the town for the new boutique. There were few African-American-owned businesses there, which made her store, Alythia, something of a novelty and provided her with a delightful profit. Not to mention a getaway.

The girls knew she had opened the Aspen boutique but not that she'd secured digs there, as well. The condo commanded a hefty portion of her earnings, but it was an investment that had proved worthwhile. The condominium was in the same building as her store and served as a home to those who visited Aspen frequently throughout the year. Aly didn't know if her workload would require such extensive travel, but she hoped that it would.

While the building's first floor was home to such establishments as bookstores, eateries, boutiques and salons, the upper floors were dedicated to high-end condominiums. All areas provided splendid views of rolling hills of white that were often dotted by tracks of skis and snowboards, which trekked across the fresh powder on and off throughout the day and much of the night.

The place was the epitome of serenity whether it was teeming with snow seekers or was bereft of bodies, with only the waves of snowy hillsides and distant white-capped mountains. The place had repaid her in more ways than the obvious. Her contentment. That satisfying peace of mind was at its highest whenever she spent time there, and never had she been so in need of solace.

Aly took another sip of the steamy white jasmine tea

before setting the mug on a stone end table that flanked a massive sofa, which lent a glorious vantage point for enjoying her view or the TV, whichever held her fancy. She snuggled into the thick fleece blanket that was usually thrown across the back of the sofa and nuzzled her head into the arm of the chair while she enjoyed the late-afternoon scenery.

The forecast had called for a fast-moving early-season storm that the meteorologists weren't anticipating would be much trouble. Still, fresh powder was always cause for celebration, and Alythia only wanted to hunker down and enjoy the show.

With the exception of the shallow lamplight filtering in from the short hallway leading to her bedroom, the condo was dim. That would change as the moon rose. Aly felt her eyelids grow weightier, a testament to her relaxation. She shivered, another bit of proof of her contentedness, yet Aly debated whether to grab a robe to cover the tank sleep dress she'd lounged in for the better part of the afternoon.

She noticed a heavy flake land on one of the sliding glass doors leading out to her wooden balcony. She decided the blanket and hot mug of tea suited her nicely.

She'd been watching the increasing intensity of the snowfall for about twenty minutes when a soft rap fell upon her door. She raised her head from the arm of the sofa, at first thinking she'd misheard. No one ever knocked on her door, not even her neighbors, who were spread out across the four units along the wide U-shaped corridor.

The knock came again and again and Alythia considered the camouflage-print tank gown she sported. Suddenly, the robe sounded like a great idea as she contemplated answering the door. The knock returned and she silently commanded away her silliness. Perhaps the storm was to be a bit more vicious than the forecasters had predicted.

"Coming!" she called out hastily, pushing herself up off the sofa. She grabbed the fleece blanket as an afterthought and tied it in a makeshift sarong about her waist.

As a precaution, she looked through the privacy window and jumped before going rigidly still. She snapped to after a second and then pulled open the door to stare dumbfounded into Gage's devilishly amused eyes.

Aly closed her mouth, which had fallen open upon first glimpse at who stood on the opposite side of the door. Her lips parted again as questions raced through her mind, begging to be asked. She only closed her mouth when those questions refused to leave her tongue.

Gage's smile only gained definition. "Let me help you." He moved closer.

"Gage, what are you doing here?"

He sought to mimic her by making his voice softer and overtly breathy.

The attempt took Aly's mind off her surprise and tapped into her amusement. "I don't sound like that," she insisted.

He was leaning on the doorframe, something seductively male belying his easy expression. "I can recall a few times when you've sounded exactly like that."

Cheeks burning, Alythia bowed her head and silently repeated the question he'd anticipated.

All the while, Gage relaxed against the framing, seemingly delighted in watching her as she tried to get a handle on what was going on.

* * *

He wouldn't deny the fact that he had selfishly cheered the way she'd lived her life. For that lifestyle had kept her available for him. Selfish indeed, he added grimly. It was no way to live, regardless of how he felt it had benefited him. She had brought such a feeling of contentment with her and to him without even knowing it. The least he could do was show her that living didn't mean she was unworthy.

Alythia's verbal skills returned as his thumb smoothed across her jaw. "What are you doing here?" The words tumbled out.

"You left me without saying goodbye." He set his head at a stern tilt. "I tend to take stuff like that personally."

"Gage, I'm sorry, it—"

"Tsk, tsk. Although this would be the time for apologies, I'm afraid you've worn out your welcome with all those *sorrys.* You'll have to come up with another, *better* way to get your regrets across." In case she was confused, he let his chocolaty stare travel the length of her body.

"I can't."

"Why not?" His query held a simplicity, as if he honestly had no clue about any of the drama that had befallen them over the past four days.

"I…" She licked her lips. "Are you alone?"

"Very alone." He exaggerated his disappointment with a forlorn shrug. "Sent my friends back on the plane, took another one here."

Aly smiled, seeking to make light of the moment. "You trust them not to talk your pilots into carrying them off on another adventure?"

Gage left the doorframe and Aly straightened, as well. She tilted back her head in order to maintain eye contact when he looked down at her.

"I don't give a damn where they go as long as they don't wind up here."

"I can't sleep with you," Aly virtually moaned when he cleared the door and pushed it shut.

"Can't or won't?" He rested against the closed door.

"Does it matter?" she countered.

Shrugging more casually then, Gage pulled off the hat he wore. "Really it doesn't," he said while tossing the knit cap back and forth. "Either way poses a challenge, but it's nothing I can't handle."

"Gage—"

He snagged her wrist, drew her flush against him, and the rest of her comment collapsed. She shivered instead, a fact she could have attributed to her fleece blanket tumbling to the floor or the cool leather of the black bomber jacket he'd yet to remove. Her bare skin reacted to the chill that penetrated the clingy fabric of her gown.

His mouth moved along the slim line of her neck while his hands charted a similar course along the curvaceous plane of her body. Every part of her reacted, her nipples already contracting against the leather, her sex aching for his attention. Alythia squeezed her eyes shut.

"Gage…" Her hands found their way inside his jacket to rest over a team emblem emblazoned across the sweatshirt beneath. "Wait…"

"Forget it." He let the words merge into the kiss he sought to punish her with.

Aly then lost any ability to stand, her strength abandoning her even as she labored to twist and arch herself against him while heightening the fire of her kiss. It was no matter as Gage balanced her bottom in his hands and perfectly aligned her sex with his. The fiery intensity of their kiss eventually had its strength-stealing effects on Gage.

Keeping her sealed against his tall, unyielding frame, he leaned against the door. Soft, intermittent groans resonated from his throat as he squeezed her almost unbearably close as if seeking to feel her through the barrier of his clothes.

Gage acknowledged Alythia's resistance. He ended their kiss in midthrust of his tongue and pressed his mouth to her ear. "Are you trying to tell me to stop? Alythia?" He tapped her bottom to encourage her answer.

She gave an obedient shake of her head and sent a slew of blue-black waves into her face. "Only to wait..." she managed.

His gaze was easy, sympathetic and without a shred of mercy. "Afraid I can't do that."

When he kissed her then, Aly accepted her fate. Melting, turning into a pliant mound of sensation beneath his hands, she worked at taking him out of his jacket. She didn't make much headway, preoccupied as she was by his kiss. She accomplished her task while he crossed the room, cradling her high against him. Aly was able to push the jacket from his shoulders just as he settled in the armchair that sat catercornered to the sofa.

Gage had her straddle his lap, which sent the hem of her gown rising to the crease of her thighs. The wispy panties she wore beneath the garment sent a growling obscenity from someplace deep in his throat. Kissing resumed, tongues battling fiercely as they moved feverishly, desperate to be closer. Aly whimpered, shifting her thighs when his fingertips brushed the hem of her panties' crotch.

She whimpered yet again when he withheld in giving her the caress she wanted. She dropped a playful slap across his dark, lovely face, having spied his lopsided grin. Gage, in return, brushed his fingers a little closer to the center of the garment's dampening middle.

Shameless, she raked a thumbnail across the shadow of whiskers that blessed his face with a fully dangerous and sexy appeal.

She gasped into his skillful mouth, emitting a tiny grunt. At last he ignored the barrier of material separating his fingers from her core. Desire had completely drugged her by then, and she was unable to even return the ravenous thrusts of his tongue against hers. Her mouth was a weak, circular O, suitable only to grant escape to the countless signs of satisfaction he coaxed. The slow dips and rotations of his middle finger set her femininity on a continuous moisture cycle. Greedily, Alythia rode the exploring finger, her lashes fluttering uncontrollably as she hungered for the release she knew his touch would provide.

"No…Gage, please…don't…"

He'd intentionally stopped the love he was making to her, observing her with a wry smile in place. "Are you done with wanting me to wait?"

"Yes…please, yes…" she moaned in tandem with wriggling her hips, urging his fingers into movement.

Gage braced off the back of the chair, then drew the sweatshirt up and over his head with one hand without removing the other from its naughty position. Alythia spasmed vigorously when her fingers grazed the sleek, toned wall of his chest even as her hips resumed the sensual rhythm they performed above his waist.

Gage took the time to release her hips and relieve her of the gown. The task was barely done and he was nourishing himself at her breast as though she had the power to curb his famished state. He'd removed a condom from the back pocket of his jeans and was pressing the packet into her palm. He left her to handle the necessary chore, preferring to share his attentions between her chest and her intimate folds, which were slick with the moisture her passion had conjured.

She was quivering terribly. Gage kept one breast captive in a secure yet gentle hold and subjected its nipple to infrequent rounds of suckling and insistent brushes from his thumb.

Alythia applied the protective sheath perfectly once she'd unfastened his button fly to free a stunning erection.

Gage muttered something in the neighborhood of impatience. Abandoning her breasts, he suddenly dropped his hands to her hips, lifted her and filled her with the thick proof of his virility. She had no trouble allowing him to direct her moves and chanted his name in a thankful litany.

Gage rested his head back against the chair, studying her as he worked her body to his gratification. For a time, Aly held her hands over his where they handled her hips. Then she was smoothing them over her tummy and across her rib cage. Briefly, she cupped her breasts, making him groan while bringing more potency to his already fortifying thrusts.

Once Aly moved on to thread all ten fingers through her hair, Gage indulged in more nourishment, suckling her nipples, still budded and glistening from his earlier attention. Aly wrenched out a sound fueled by pleasure and pain when his grasp on her hips took on a viselike intensity. She dropped her hands across his once more and was satisfied that they would maintain the delicious rhythm they had perfected.

Gage surrendered then, unable to uphold any promises he'd foolishly made to put his hormones on the back burner and devote himself primarily to her fulfillment. Burrowing his head into her chest, he realized that he had lived up to his promise. He could feel her climaxing, shuddering in unison with him as they submitted to waves of pleasure that rolled them in a seductive storm.

"Why'd you leave without saying goodbye to me?" Gage kissed the top of Alythia's head.

They had moved from the large armchair to the sofa, where they shared the blanket and took in the sight of the steadier snowfall. The condo was moonlit and quiet but for the minute tapping of the snowflakes against the glass doors leading out to the balcony.

"Didn't I just make up for leaving?" she asked.

He dropped another kiss to her head, gathering her impossibly close. "You definitely made up for it."

Alythia discovered she had been wrong. She'd only *thought* she'd known true contentment lounging there alone on her sofa. But *this* was it and if it wasn't, it was certainly a damn sight closer than she'd been a few hours ago. She didn't want anything to infringe on that and curved into Gage as she tried to will away the conversation.

"Why'd you go, Alythia?"

"You know how it is," she huffed. "Work to do…"

"Right, business worries *can* make you forget everything."

Regret forced Aly to close her eyes. She didn't want him to think that her work was enough to make her forget him. "Coming here was all I could do to forget everything that went on back there, Gage."

"That's got nothing to do with us, Alythia." His arms about her tightened in sync with the hardening of his voice.

"I can't understand how you can feel that way." She clenched a fist to the center of his chest and held it there. "These are people we'll have to see all the time."

"Not necessarily."

"Are you suggesting we dump our friends?" Her tone was playful.

"Not at all, but it'd be hard to get tugged into crap if we aren't around."

Aly braced herself on an elbow and gaped down at him. "Are you talking about not going back?"

"Yeah…" He shrugged as though the plan were perfectly logical.

Alythia couldn't believe what she was hearing and that fact was amplified as she studied him with a look of amused disbelief. Gage graced her with a roguish wink and tucked her back between his arm and chest.

"Look at that snow," he marveled, and put another kiss to the top of her head.

Chapter 12

"You live here?" Aly figured more words would fail her as she stood just inside the grand corner condo.

The place occupied the opposite end of her floor. There were only two of the L-shaped units, one at either end of the hall. Alythia had considered herself blessed to have acquired the spot she had and often wondered about the kind of people who could afford digs on such a scale and rarely use them.

Gage kept his place leaning on the condo's open door, arms folded over a lightweight burgundy hoodie. He seemed more interested in watching her observe his home than in the place itself.

Aly was drawn to the wall of glass that filled the far right and rear wall of the living room. The scene before her eyes was stunning and provided an almost panoramic view that was impossibly more spectacular than her own.

"How long have you lived here?"

"Let's see…" Gage focused on something in the distance. "Since yesterday." He smiled when she turned on him with an exasperated look. "I had to be sure I'd have somewhere to stay if you decided not to let me into your place last night."

Alythia was on the verge of laughter. "And I guess all the hotels in Aspen were full?"

"Anegada spoiled me." He shrugged. "I'm used to being close to where you are now, I guess."

"All in the span of a few days." She shook her head. "This is a pretty penny to drop on a place you'll never use."

He eased his hands into the pockets of his navy carpenter's pants and frowned over her prediction. "Why do you think I won't use it?"

"Do you have business here?"

"Sure do." He shut the door, rested back against it. "I was at work all night last night."

"Be serious." Alythia fought against smiling and failed.

"I am."

Her smile wavered. "Don't tell me you bought this place for me?"

"Would that scare you?"

The quiet seriousness of his voice held Alythia speechless for a moment. She didn't know what to make of the steady gaze or easy stance next to the door, with which he beckoned her.

"You don't know me, Gage."

"I'm trying to fix that."

"Why?"

"Why not?"

Aroused, exasperated, angry at herself for not trusting that *he* was so right for her, she rolled her eyes and turned back to observe her understatedly plush surroundings.

Gage dropped his easy expression. In its place emerged uncertainty. For the thousandth time since he'd taken off after her, he asked himself what the hell he thought he was doing. He wasn't unaware of his manner with women. Truth be told, his reputation wasn't much better than that of his closest friends, but such things only elevated a man's appeal, didn't they?

Unfair or not, women always fared far worse in the blows dealt to their reputations. It was an unfailing truth, whether the blows were earned or inherited. He'd toyed with reconsidering the Aspen trip, telling himself that he was in for an uphill battle.

Regardless of its awesomeness, he knew that she'd regretted sleeping with him in Anegada. That regret had probably carried over to what had happened between them the night before, as well.

And what about himself? He considered. Did he now imagine himself in love with her because of the mindblowing sex they'd enjoyed? No...that wasn't why he was there. Of that he was certain. The final hours of the Anegada trip were prime examples of hell in a handbasket. Such a beautiful environment tainted by such ugliness. Yet all he could think of while keeping the offending parties separated was how badly he craved the contentment Alythia's presence provided him. She'd been an anchor in a storm and he had fallen in love with her.

There was a knock at the door. Alythia watched as Gage answered. He admitted a small man dressed in dark trousers with a white shirt and a bow tie. The man brought with him a square table set for two and carrying silver platters with coffee and juice carafes.

The server smiled in Alythia's direction as he pulled the covers from the platters to reveal steaming dishes of fluffy scrambled eggs with pancakes, bacon and fruit.

"So, then, your brother-in-law is the epitome of the perfect man?" Gage asked.

She and Gage were halfway through their filling breakfast. They had discussed Gage's upbringing as an only child and being without cousins, as his parents were only children, as well. Alythia sat riveted by stories of family vacations to Spain and Africa—places she could scarcely imagine as a child. When it was her turn to share, she couldn't help but feel a little self-conscious about her humdrum upbringing. Gage, however, seemed completely absorbed in her stories. Encouraged, Alythia felt more engaged as her talk moved to her older sister's true-love tale.

"She wouldn't agree that Owen's the perfect man but… Well, the girl's always been a little silly." Aly joined in laughing with Gage at her sister's expense.

"He does stay busy, though." Alythia relaxed in her chair and sipped at her almond coffee. "Life of a lawyer, I guess."

"Wait a minute." Gage's eyes narrowed suspiciously. "Is your bother-in-law Owen Hays? The attorney?"

"That's him." Alythia beamed.

"I've seen your sister." He regarded Aly with heightened appraisal. "I'm thinking her husband is *very* devoted to her." He placed a finger alongside his temple. "Your parents shared an awesome gene pool with their girls."

"Thank you." She nodded, gracefully accepting the compliment. "But it's not just good genes that caught Owen's eye. Angela did everything right."

"How so?"

Feeling rejuvenated by the fabulous breakfast and the wintry view, Aly didn't mind talking. "She was just a great example. No one *told* her to be. I guess she felt like she had to be for me, the baby. There weren't many shining examples where we're from…." She placed her mug on the table and propped her chin on the back of her hand.

"Making sacrifices and walking good paths…they aren't things people just do because others need or expect it. There has to be a real good deep-down reason that gives them the ability to see it all through."

As she confided to him, her amethyst stare alight with love and admiration for her sister, she imagined that Gage must have been wondering how much of that "real good deep-down" *she* had.

"Angie already had four years under her belt as a prosecutor—a damn good one—before she met Owen. She'd worked hard enough to call her own shots, but working that hard doesn't leave much time to develop relationships." Aly shrugged her brows. "Good thing for her, too—helped her live up to that lofty goal of saving herself for marriage."

"You think that's why Owen was interested?" Gage leaned closer, resting both elbows on the table.

"Isn't that what all men want?" Alythia averted her eyes. "To be the first and the last?"

"Some men only care about being the last." An animal intensity sharpened his features. "You only care about that when you've found the right one."

Aly wouldn't let herself fall under the spell that his liquid gaze was wholly capable of weaving. "It was obvious to Owen that Angela was the right one." Her intention had been to keep the conversation on funny family stories, but she found herself discarding the decision.

"How'd you find me, Gage? Why?"

"I put my already overworked assistant to work on it, got my results fast," he told her at last.

Aly nodded, following the invisible design her fingers traced on the tablecloth. "Are you used to getting your results quickly?"

"In some things."

"Business?"

"Always."

"Women?"

"Frequently."

"You forgot one," he said when it seemed she was done with her questions. "Things that matter," he supplied.

Aly regarded him curiously. "Doesn't your business matter?"

"Things that last, then."

"What's your track record there? With things that last?"

"Not sure," he responded, but he looked uncertain. "I never went after anything I truly cared about lasting."

"Your business—"

"Business isn't even in the same hemisphere as this, Alythia."

She ducked her head, trying to soothe her uncertainties about the words she was about to utter. "Why'd you come to find me, Gage? You and I enjoyed Anegada for the most part. There would've been no harm in letting it end there. Considering…"

"You're right." Absently, he stirred at the honey butter that had been left behind following their breakfast. "I guess a big part of that enjoyment is what brought me out here. A big part, but not even half of it."

"How long can you stay?" Suddenly she wasn't altogether sure that she wanted to know the other part of what brought Gage Vincent to her doorstep.

"I'm the boss." He reclined in his chair again. "I can stay for as long as I want."

"And what of your overworked assistant?" Her smile was playfully judgmental.

"It'll be good for him to be in charge for a little longer. Besides, I've got him at work on closing a pretty big deal. I shouldn't get back too soon and have the poor guy thinking the boss is micromanaging."

Alythia laughed, though she was all too aware of the "deal" Gage's assistant was most likely trying to close.

"Thank you for this." She cast an appreciative look around the room. "I, um…I really do need to check on things at the boutique."

He nodded. "Dinner later? We'll go out." He chuckled, correctly reading the smile she returned. "We'll be around lots of low drama, I promise."

"Gosh…not even a lovers' spat?"

"*Especially* not a lovers' spat."

"It's a date!" Aly threw back her head to laugh again.

She caught the sheer heat flooding Gage's eyes as he only watched her.

"I should go." She pushed out of her seat. "This was really nice."

Alythia stood while Gage continued to recline in his chair. She was passing him when he snagged her wrist and tugged her down into a kiss that grew wet and needy in a second. Aly was moaning weakly and entwining her tongue around his in a lazy tangle before she bit his lip softly and repeated the erotic action. She was in his lap a moment later.

Willpower was nonexistent where Gage was concerned, and she could accept that. In his arms, she could imagine that they could be more. It didn't matter that reality screamed they could be nothing more than a fling.

Gage patted her hip, broke the kiss to drop one behind her ear. "I'll see you later," he whispered.

It was no small feat for Aly to draw herself away, but she managed. She made a dash for the door before she said to hell with business and uncertainty and returned to take what she wanted from him.

Outside his door, she rested back to slow her breathing and was summoned from her haze by the chiming of her phone. Marianne. Alythia changed her mind about answering. Casting a lingering look across her shoulder at Gage's door, she turned and sprinted down the hallway toward her own.

Charlotte, NC

"Great," Marianne Young whispered when her call went to voice mail. She considered hanging up and then decided to give her client the news Mari guessed Aly-thia had been dreading.

"Aly, it's Mari. Looks like Jeena was right. Gage Vincent *is* the silent power hovering over the new down-town space. Call me. We should discuss how you want to handle it. Talk to you soon."

Marianne ended the call only to have the phone ring less than a minute later. "Aly?" she greeted without checking the faceplate.

"Webster Reese," a deep voice countered.

"Oh! I—I'm sorry." Marianne collapsed back into her desk chair.

"I'm the one who should apologize, Ms. Young."

"Oh?"

Webb chuckled at her bewildered tone. "I didn't mean to upset you the other day when I called for in-formation on your client Alythia Duffy."

"Oh…Mr. Reese." Marianne remembered then. "It's okay—"

"No, it's not, and I apologize a lot better in person."

"Mr.—Mr. Reese, are you…asking me out?" Mari leaned forward in her chair, threading fingers through her reddish-brown bangs. "That's really not necessary and it probably wouldn't be a good idea anyway."

"Oh?" Webb let his bewilderment show.

Mari cringed. "We're, um…we're kind of caught up in a business deal."

"Business?" Webb's bewilderment showed no signs of waning.

"My client's trying to secure retail space in a build-ing your boss owns. We've submitted a bid and every-thing."

"Yuck. I take it our bosses don't know any of this."

"Just told mine via voice mail."

"Ouch." Webb followed up with a grunt. "I think I'll just stay a little too busy to inform my boss."

Marianne cringed again. "He won't take it well, I guess?"

"I can't say, Ms. Young, but something tells me that *I* don't want to be the one to tell him."

"Dammit..." Alythia had just replayed Marianne's message in hopes of hearing a different version and had not gotten her wish.

Perhaps she *was* making a mountain out of a molehill. Maybe it wouldn't rattle Gage in the least to discover that the woman he was seeing wanted space in a prime piece of real estate that he owned. Maybe he wouldn't think that she'd been sleeping with him to better her chances at securing it.

Maybe he wouldn't think that—if she hadn't slept with him two days after meeting him.

"Stop, Aly." She tried to focus on getting ready for dinner. The comb stilled in her hand and she studied it through the mirror without really seeing it. Then she was hurling the wide-toothed instrument across the room and holding her head in her hands when it hit the wall.

Chapter 13

The Soup Niche lived up to its name as a popular locale for the most savory soups and stews in the area. While its menu downplayed the obvious, the Niche held equal appeal for the high-end jet-setters and college-aged X Gamers who frequented the area. It was a place that made a person feel right at home and it was exactly what Alythia needed that night.

She and Gage had opted for jeans and bulky sweatshirts instead of more casual-chic attire, both of which were in fine form at the Niche. Between drinks, appetizers and the main course, Aly had taken off her gray hiking boots and tucked her legs beneath her on the oversize gold armchair she occupied at their table for two.

"Is this okay?"

Aly shook her head when he grinned. "You know it

is." She looked around at the dining room, fire lit courtesy of the wild flames licking the wide hearths that occupied various corners of the cozily designed room. "I haven't had the chance to come here before. I definitely won't forget it."

"Neither will I." Gage gave a pointed look toward a few high-enders who had decided on a more upscale style of dress to enjoy their soup dinner in.

"They're only being respectful of the food." Aly inhaled the intermingling of aromas.

"Never thought of it that way." He shrugged while slathering a roll with an obscene amount of butter. "I'd rather pay my respects to the food by eating it."

"Agreed." Aly raised her spoon in a mock toast and then followed suit when Gage dug into a deep bowl of hearty beef stew.

They were completing their second bowl of stew from their personal soup tureen set in the center of the table when the server arrived to replace their empty beer pitcher with a fresh full one.

Gage settled back to study his date while the waiter supplied their refills. His cocoa stare maintained a knowing frequency as he watched Alythia, who had grown increasingly quiet as the food disappeared. Once the waiter had finished with the refills, Gage reached for his chilled mug and helped himself to a healthy swig.

"Gage? I need to tell you something."

He smiled. "Okay."

"I got a call from Charlotte."

Gage's mug hit the table with a thud that sent the beer sloshing up over the mouth of the glass. The liquid coated his hand.

"Calm down." Aly reached over to dab a napkin at his wet skin. "It's not about our friends—it's about business."

Gage took the napkin and handled the task of drying his hand. His movements were virtually mechanical, his gaze curiously expectant.

"The call was from my business manager. She's been working to help me secure a spot in the downtown area." Aly pushed her bowl aside and then laced her fingers on the table. "Word is it's a building that *you* own."

His expression revealed nothing. "How do you know it's mine?"

"I didn't…at first, but my manager's very good at her job. When your assistant called trying to help you find me…well, it wasn't too hard to connect the dots."

"How long have you known this?" Gage maintained his unreadable expression.

"I swear I only found out this afternoon." Aly brought her clasped hands to her chest. "Marianne left a message but I—I didn't listen to it right away."

"Alythia." He measured the nervous excitement in her eyes. "Honey, it's your turn to calm down."

"But I never intended to deceive you with this."

He reached over to pull one of her hands from her chest. "Alythia, stop. It's all right."

"It is?" She blinked.

"Exactly what did you expect me to say or do?" He looked toward the hand clutching the front of her emerald-green sweatshirt. "Did you think I'd call you names and leave on the first flight back to Charlotte?"

"Something like that." She pressed her lips together

and then shook her head. "Aren't you at least a *little* pissed that we…have this thing between us?"

"It seems like we always have things between us. Honestly, I'd rather it be about business than our friends."

"Agreed," she sighed, though her expression and the weakness of her voice said otherwise.

Gage fidgeted with the stem of the once-frosted mug. "People say I'm good at what I do because I'm patient."

"I may've heard that somewhere." She smiled.

"I don't know how that could be totally true when I'm possessive as hell." His gaze was level and unwavering toward her. "I say all that to get you to understand that I don't plan on walking away from this or roaring at you for thinking you had deceived me. If that's what you were banking on, you probably shouldn't have told me you'd discovered that news in the first place."

She gave him an appraising nod. "So there *is* a way to rile your temper. I was starting to wonder."

"You have no idea." His smirk was equal parts amusement and ferocity.

Aly gave in to her laughter then. "These have been the strangest days of my life. I didn't have any intentions of falling in love when I went to Anegada, only to build my stores and have a little fun if time permitted. Then not only do two of my friends get caught up in unbelievable drama in the span of a few hours, but another goes from being adored by her fiancé to being hit by him." She brought her elbows to the table and cupped her hands around her face. "How'd I get so damned lucky?"

Alythia's playfully exasperated tone went unnoticed by Gage, who'd heard little else following her mention of falling in love. He wondered whether she meant it or if she'd simply been using it to describe how close they were becoming.

Her grin weakened. "Things are moving very fast."

"Too fast for you?" he asked.

"I don't know." She laughed. "Not much compares to what's been going on. I think it scares me a little."

"Do *I* scare you?"

"If you were any other man…perhaps."

His gaze faltered to the tablecloth. "Why do you suppose that is?"

"It could have a lot to do with your money and who you are."

"But no?" His tone was hopeful, as if he sensed there was more she wanted to add. "What?" he pressed when she shook her head.

"Discussing this might put us in forbidden territory," she warned.

"I can take it."

"All right. It has to do with your friends."

"Forget I asked."

She laughed softly. "You really care a lot about them."

"And I don't know if that's an asset or a flaw."

"It's admirable." She laughed again when he snorted.

Gage slumped back in his chair and worked his fingers over the cap of sleek brown covering his head. "The last few days have been like straws breaking my back and it's weird because I never cared before." His lone dimpled smile was one of surprise.

"Issues like this creep up often anytime we get together. Somebody says the wrong thing to a woman, somebody's seen with a woman and called out by *an-*

other woman, who thought she was the only one.... Our screwups are infinite." He patted a hand to his chest. "I'm including my own screwups in there, Alythia."

"And here we are." Again she scanned the golden-lit dining room. "We've known each other all of four days and you really believe you can stay here in Aspen and turn your back on your life in Carolina."

"Do you remember what I said about being patient?" He watched her give a slow nod. "There's a lot going through my head about us right now. One thing I do know is that I want to know you and that's gonna take time, given my own...reputation. It'll probably take a lot of time."

The server returned to clear away some of their dishes. Gage and Alythia waited patiently, silently absorbing all that had been said during the course of their meal.

"We've already skipped ahead several steps," Gage continued once the waiter had moved on. "Guess that doesn't go a long way in proving my rep isn't well deserved."

"Hmph. And *I* guess that can go double for me."

"Why?" He inclined his head. "Why should it go double for you?"

"Please don't try and pretend you don't know." She grinned broadly. "It always goes double for women. Sex, business—the standards are always double."

"So would you have a problem if we scrapped the standards?"

Aly stretched languidly in her chair. "I'd *love* to scrap the standards."

"Think we can?" His rich, chocolaty stare narrowed.

"Sure." Her demeanor was cool yet a tad cynical.

"As long as we stay in our own private corner here in Aspen like you've suggested."

"But that's not reality, is it?" Gage sighed as though he were reluctantly turning himself toward that very mode of thinking.

"We'll have to face it sooner or later, you know? I'd rather face it before things between us get too…complex."

Gage kept his thoughts silent, admitting that things between them were already "too complex" as far as he was concerned. He knew if she were to ask that they end things right there, he'd do everything in his power to persuade her to change her mind.

"Will you come back to Charlotte with me?" he asked.

"There're still some things I need to check in on at the shop, but I could—"

"No, Alythia…I'm asking if you'll come back *with* me."

Understanding pooled in her extraordinary eyes. "With you. *With* you, with you? Like…we're a couple?"

A teasing wince softened his features adorably. "I promise it won't be as bad as you're making it sound."

"Are we gonna be met by a slew of reporters and paparazzi?"

His laughter drew attention and that was no surprise. The sound was hearty, genuine and oftentimes quite contagious.

"I promise I don't merit that kind of confusion."

Aly still appeared doubtful. "I don't know.… I do my best not to draw attention."

"And I'm happy about that but you're too damn beautiful to stay in the shadows and too damn beautiful to venture out there alone." He tugged the sleeve of her shirt. "I've got faith in you and if all this goes to hell, we always have Aspen."

"Or Anegada." Aly reached for her mug and raised it in toast.

Gage laughed again and reciprocated her gesture. "That'll make Clive a happy man," he predicted.

After dinner Gage and Alythia strolled the village, which was a forest of white following the previous day's storm and the light dusting from earlier that day. Alythia kept a tight grip on the arm Gage offered, and not so much out of a need for steadiness, she silently admitted as they navigated the wintry streets.

It was the sheer pleasure of being close. The warmth and security radiating from his tall, lean frame heightened her need at every level. She smoothed her hands over his biceps. The unyielding hardness of it was in no way diminished by the heavy jacket or sweatshirt worn beneath.

Alythia gave a quick laugh when she realized they had crossed the block where her boutique was located. "I didn't know we'd already walked so far. That's my shop there." She pointed toward a storefront boasting a snow-dusted gold canopy and French double doors.

"Take me for a tour?" Gage asked, smiling when she tugged his arm and led them across the lightly trafficked street.

Aly made quick work of unlocking the door and deactivating the alarms. Leaving the blinds closed, she hit the panel for the recessed lighting along the polished hardwood floors and drop ceiling of carved maple wood. The scant illumination added an effective gold dousing to the boutique's main level.

"It's very simple." She smiled contentedly and added a flourishing wave. "I'm still getting a feel for the place."

"Simple is good." Gage strolled the area, taking in the coziness created by mock Queen Anne chairs and love seats. He appeared drawn to the rows of clothing, paying specific attention to the array of frilly garments.

"Why don't you wear this stuff?" His gaze was on the lingerie he fingered.

"I wear it all the time." Clasping her hands at her back, she slowly approached the lingerie section. "You've only known me a week, remember. Not much time to display my entire wardrobe," she joked.

He nodded, eyes still fixed on the delicates. "What's upstairs?" he asked.

"Office and fitting room." She looked toward a spiraling brass staircase.

"Give me a private showing?"

"Ha! You've been getting those all week."

"Not like this." He waved a few of the pieces he'd taken a great liking to.

"I beg to differ," she still argued.

Gage continued to wave his preferences. "But the customer is always right, right?"

"Are you in the market for lingerie, Mr. Vincent?"

"I'm in the market for lingerie with you in it."

"A showing, then?"

"A showing."

Alythia accepted the pieces he offered and then led the way up the wide oak stairs secured by the brown framework. The stairway opened up into an elegant yet comfortably furnished fitting area. With the press of another button, lighting was activated from stout black lamps that occupied the middles of glass tables next to deep butter suede armchairs along the rear wall of the room.

"The boutique doesn't make a habit of modeling, sir," she teasingly informed him, "not even for customers such as yourself."

He caught her elbow and pulled her to him when she would have moved past. "What kind of customer am I?"

"Persuasive…and a little intense."

He wrinkled his nose and Aly felt her heart flip over the guileless affect the gesture cast across his gorgeous features.

"That makes me sound scary."

"Not the vibe I get at all." She moved closer with every word he uttered. Their lips were but a breath apart when she pulled away.

"Over here are our dressing rooms." Her manner was breezy as she waved her hands to direct his attention. "Seating areas are here, as well as our coffee-and-Danish nook. Though they're closed right now due to the time." Her smile was playfully apologetic.

"What's there?" He looked toward a small hallway just beyond the fitting rooms.

"My office suite." She motioned to the garments he'd selected. "Do you have a preference?"

"Definitely."

She feigned distaste at his one-track mind even though he had every part of her body set on tingle. "Please choose, sir." She gave the lingerie another shake.

He did so obediently, cocking his head to the left to

indicate his choice. Alythia turned for the rooms. She didn't get far. He had her flush against him the instant she was within reach. He was crushing her mouth beneath his tongue, thrusting, exploring, branding.

Alythia moaned without shame, hungrily engaging in the sultry duel. One hand hung limp at her side, the garments she grasped threatening a descent to the floor as the hold weakened. With her free hand she massaged his nape, her glossy nails just grazing the soft hair tapering there.

"Hey?" She managed to draw back, sliding her finger to outline the alluring curve of his mouth. "You wanted a showing, didn't you?" She easily sensed his reluctance in releasing her and left him with a saucy wink before sauntering to one of the fitting rooms.

Needing something, anything, to keep his mind off of her naked and less than twenty feet away, Gage took his own personal tour of the area. He thought of how very much the space reflected Alythia's personality—airy yet with a warm tug that enhanced the contentment he was coming to cherish about her. It was a place that enveloped its guests in a cocoon of welcome.

"Those chairs are to die for!" Aly called out from the dressing room. "They'll put you to sleep if you're not careful!" She was hanging the strap of her bra to one of the room's satin padded hooks when his arms snaked about her waist. Her legs went to water, his hands smothering her breasts as his mouth brushed her ear.

"Guess I'll have to find something to keep me up, then."

"I…don't allow this sort of thing in here, Mr. Vincent." Her voice was a breathy whisper. She let her head rest back against his shoulder.

"What sort of thing?" He plied her with examples, his thumbs flicking her nipples until the buds protruded. As he fondled her steadily, his unoccupied hand drifted down the lithe, lovely line of her body. Briefly, he fingered her naval, smiling when she wriggled insistently.

Aly bowed her head, biting her lip while a flurry of sensation engulfed her. Weakly, her hands covered his at her breasts, and she nuzzled her back against his chest, luxuriating in his strength.

Gage suckled her earlobe, his fingers skirting the lacy waistband of the charcoal-gray panties she wore. "Open your eyes, Alythia."

His command was soft, effectively coaxing her cooperation. She watched as his fingers disappeared inside the wispy material at her hips, nudging them lower the deeper his hand journeyed. Her lashes fluttered.

"Don't you do it." His command was firm that time. The hand at her breast flexed, giving her a tiny jerk to encourage her to oblige.

In the dressing room mirror, she watched as the panties she wore were pulled to her upper thighs, leaving her most private asset bared to his gaze. Gage smoothed the back of his hand across the bare triangle of flesh above her femininity. Dually attentive, he launched a slow nibbling of her shoulder.

"Don't do it…" he ordered, more playfully that time when he saw her lashes fluttering as he gnawed her satiny skin.

Alythia was desperate to shimmy out of the panties and turn to face him. Gage denied that with another flex around the breast he molested. She was left no choice but to stand and witness the play of emotion across her face when his thumb stroked the bud of hypersensitive flesh at the apex of her thighs.

An orgasm-promising spasm rippled through her, helped along by his constant manipulation of her nipples, which seemed to cry out for attention, given their erectness.

Alythia watched her mouth slacken beneath the weight of desire as he intensified the caress to her clit while thrusting his middle finger high, deep inside and then rotating and giving her leave to enjoy the treat, wildly uninhibited.

She murmured his name, turning her head while feverishly brushing the panties down her legs and off of her ankles. She was panting, her mouth desperately seeking his. Unmindful of his instructions against turning, she did just that and without ever breaking the kiss they shared.

Moments later Gage had her in his arms and was carrying her from the fitting area and down the short corridor that led to her office. Inside, there was no need for light. Mutual desire guided their fingertips. She began to undress him. Gage offered his assistance only when she took too long with the button fly of his jeans.

She led him to the sofa, her intention to straddle him and greedily put him inside her. Gage's intentions differed. The second he felt the sofa, he put Alythia on her back beneath him. She could hear the belt buckle at his jeans clink as the denims were roused. Gage made quick work of checking his pockets for the condoms he'd pushed inside them earlier that night.

Alythia was glad he hadn't requested her assistance,

for she didn't think she had the strength to perform the task of securing their protection. Those concerns happily vanished when she felt him spreading her, filling her to the hilt with him. Instantly, her hips lifted into a gentle writhe, stirring sensation for them both.

Then came the familiar sounds of moisture squelching produced by their coupling. Gage kept one of Alythia's thighs pressed to the wide sofa. He set the other high, opening her to a deeper plundering with his thick erection. Ego-soothing arrogance rested beneath possession as he took pleasure in the sighs and cries he forced past her mouth.

Gage emitted his own sighs of abandon. His handsome dark face was sheltered in the crook of her neck, where muffled groans of satisfaction were buried. Without warning, he pulled Aly to her desk, where he positioned her and took her from behind.

The darkened room was brought to life by their mingled gasps and groans of delight. Gage dragged wet kisses between Alythia's shoulder blades, marking the line of her spine with his tongue. He covered her breasts in his hands, pulling her back against him while his thrusts claimed a lovely savagery. Alythia could scarcely catch her breath, but words of complaint had fled her vocabulary. What remained of their evening passed in a lusty blur.

Chapter 14

"Well, what's this?" Alythia murmured, crossing her bare legs and resting an elbow on her knee in order to lift her mobile to a more comfortable viewing level.

Gage shook his head and grinned, not bothering to turn when he heard her across the bedroom. They had finally gotten around to christening his condo. "Let me guess," he called from where he stood preparing two coffees. "Our destination calls?"

"It's a text. Orchid wants to see me."

"About the wedding?"

Aly was stunned. "Do you still think there's gonna be one?"

"It'd be somethin' to see." His torso shook when he chuckled.

"Well, I guess I really should touch base with everybody." Aly returned her attention to the phone. "I only told Jeena I need to get away but I didn't tell her where I was going."

Gage crossed to the bed and handed her one of the steaming mugs of coffee he'd poured from the portable coffeemaker in the bedroom alcove. "They don't know you have a boutique here?"

"Oh, they do." Aly tightened her grip on the mug and straightened the pillows at her back. "But not that I have a condo here or that I've even thought about moving here."

"Have you really considered that?" He joined her on the bed. "You could be that far away from your sister? Your only family?"

"I think Angie would be happy about it." Aly warmed her hands around the mug. "All the sacrifices she made to keep me on the straight and boring path and still I become best friends with the very influences she tried to steer me clear of." She grimaced then, sending wavy swirls into her face when she bowed her head.

"That's not fair." She sipped the perfectly sweetened and creamed coffee. "I don't know what motivated Orchid or even Myrna but I do know Jeena didn't set out to become what she is."

"But we can't all run boutiques, can we?" Gage reclined on his side of the bed with his arms folded over his bare chest.

"We both dreamed of being businesswomen, since we were kids." Her expression softened with memory. "For me it was the clothes and the attitude, hmph, and then I realized that it *was* just about clothes for me. It went deeper for Jeena, though." Aly lowered her mug and set it on the night table.

"She always said she wanted to make things better

for people. Though she didn't mean in a sexual way,"
Aly tacked on ruefully. "She didn't have a hard-nosed
sister to push her the way I did. Right out of high school
she went to work for a telemarketing firm."

Aly laughed suddenly. "Jeena *really* loved it. I've
never met anyone who *really* loved telemarketing but
she did. She really was great at it because she honestly
believed in what she was doing." Easing down on the
gargantuan sleigh bed, Aly relaxed on the pillows.

"She started researching and trying to learn all she
could about starting her own firm, but things… They
just veered off track."

"How?" Gage took her hand and began to toy with
her fingers.

"One of the supervisors asked Jeena to set him up
with one of the floor operators. Jeena said he felt comfortable enough to ask her because she'd been talking
his ear off about all that telemarketing research she'd
been doing." She smiled when Gage tickled her palm.

"Turned out…telemarketing wasn't the operator's
only job and she point-blank told Jeen that it was gonna
cost the man."

"Let me guess—he paid?"

"Passed the funds right through Jeena and the rumored madam was born."

Gage could only shake his head in wonder.

"We have our faults, but I love those wenches." Her
mouth began to tremble. "I only wonder if we're good
for each other anymore. All we do lately is fight."

"I can relate to that." Gage set his head deep in the
pillows and stared up at the ceiling. "A wise man once
said the best way to stay friends is to stay away from
each other."

"So sad." Still, Alythia burst into laughter.

"But true," Gage added when his laughter had subsided.

"And sometimes necessary."

"Yeah…"

Gage continued to stare up at the ceiling without really seeing it.

"Do you think you'll have to have that kind of conversation with any of your friends?"

"Maybe one." He mopped his hands over his face and groaned. "Maybe all…"

"Maybe we all should've thought twice about that trip."

A grim smile curved Gage's mouth. "Would've been helpful if Jay and Orchid thought twice before letting their families push them into a phony marriage. I don't think they were ready for a relationship, let alone a marriage."

"And what about us?" Alythia hesitated. "Do you think *we're* ready?"

"Well, we definitely didn't have the time to find out in Anegada."

There was no laughter and Gage squeezed Aly's hand, giving a tug to encourage her closer. "In Anegada I was very much infatuated with you," he said when she was tucked into him.

"And here?"

"Coming to Aspen was about satisfying my possessive streak." He felt her sharp inhale, knowing the confession had stirred her. He cupped her chin, squeezing until she met his warm stare.

"Wanting to *stay* in Aspen is my patient streak kicking in and telling me you're a woman to wait on for however long it takes."

"That could take a long time. Lots could happen in all that time." She squeezed the hand still holding hers. "Given our brief history, chances are high that a lot *will* happen."

"I believe we can survive it." He kissed the back of her hand.

"You're putting a lot of trust in the fates."

"I'm putting a lot of trust in us."

He kissed her then, sweetly at first. Aly changed all that with the sigh she gave while arching into him.

"Nervous?"

"Probably not as much as I should be." Aly sighed as she studied a spectacular view from her seat on Gage's jet a few days later.

"We're going home." He pulled her up from the seat. "What could possibly go wrong?"

Alythia dissolved into laughter. "You're a funny guy."

"Funny but sexy. Makes all the difference."

She melted. "Yes, it does…." His words had turned her boneless. Any lingering pangs of nervousness evaporated when he jerked her into a throaty kiss. Gage brought her onto the long seat on the other side of the bar and positioned her in a straddle on his lap.

Aly wanted to feel his skin beneath her fingertips and was all too anxious to relieve him of the shirt he wore loose at the collar and hanging outside his olive-green trousers. She had time only to unbutton his shirt and splay her hands wide across the sleek plane of his chest before he turned the tables and put her beneath him on the luxurious surface of the seat.

"Take off your shirt," she murmured against his jaw, taking delight in the smooth, flawless surface though she silently admitted to missing the display of whiskers he'd sported since the Caribbean. She felt him go still against her and then his head fell to her chest.

"Gage?" She waited and then kissed his temple. "What? What's wrong?"

"I won't do this here, not here of all places."

Aly barely needed a second to understand his point and realize that she agreed. "Guess this jet does have a few too many memories."

Gage lifted his head and propped her chin on his fist. "I can promise you we'll definitely make memories of our own, but not just yet."

Her bright eyes sparkled. "You've got me curious." She curled her fingers into his collar and studied their surroundings. "You think our memories can top the ones already in circulation?"

"Lady, you have no idea." Gage gnawed her neck until she begged him to be merciful.

The day was sunny and bright if just a tad nippy when Alythia and Gage deplaned in Charlotte late that afternoon. Gage nudged her when he heard the sigh she expelled over the scene that greeted them. No reporters or paparazzi, only airport personnel and two town cars waiting on the tarmac.

"Told you I wasn't *that* important."

"Mmm…probably the calm before the storm."

They cleared the mobile staircase and Gage escorted her to one of the two town cars.

"Hey, Rich."

"Mr. V." A tall, broadly built man greeted Gage with a vigorous handshake. "Everything's in the trunk. We're all set."

"Sounds good. Take Ms. Duffy anywhere she needs to go."

"Gage, no," Aly whispered, turning to pat his cheek. "I don't need all this. I drove my car out here, remember?"

"I had your car sent back. It's waiting with a full tank in your driveway."

"This is great service."

He dipped his head. "We only aim to please." He took advantage of the closeness to inhale her subtle perfume. "Thanks, Rich," he said without looking in his driver's direction. "I'll call you, all right?" he told Alythia once Rich was settling in behind the driver's seat.

Aly was frowning, her fingertips gaining more purchase as they clutched Gage's shirt. "You're not coming with me?"

"I'm guessing you've got a lot to do." He outlined her mouth with his thumb.

It was true, but just then Aly was thinking only of how very much she'd like to go anywhere they could make love.

Gage kissed her cheek subtly, following the gesture with a pat to her hip. "Go handle your business. I'll handle mine."

"When will you call me?" She couldn't help it. She didn't want them to part ways.

He smiled, brushed another kiss across her cheek. "Not very long. Promise."

They shared another spontaneously heated kiss

and then Gage was bundling her into the town car and knocking on the hood to send the driver on his way.

"Miss Orchid will be down soon. May I get you anything else, Miss Aly?"

Alythia smiled and held the teacup closer to her chest. "No, thanks, Sienna, the tea is fine," she told the Benjamins' housekeeper. Alythia was a bit relieved to wait a little longer to chat with her friend. Like her work, the discussion was another in a long line of activities that would keep her mind off Gage.

It'd been a week and she hadn't heard from him. At first Alythia criticized herself for being surprised by that. After all, they had known each other for only a brief span of time. Was she still so naive as to believe he'd truly fallen as deeply as she wanted to think? Was she so naive to believe that he had fallen as deeply as she had?

Then another possibility occurred to her. Maybe he didn't believe she had fallen as deeply as *he* had. Perhaps this was his attempt at giving her the time to decide whether she was ready to accept what he was offering.

Truth be told, Alythia admitted she hadn't really given Gage much reason to believe that she was ready. She guessed he was leaving it to her to decide and she smiled into her teacup. Now she only needed to manage a tea party with Orchid and hope the discussion wouldn't wage too much war on her nerves.

"Alythia, girl!"

Aly noted she wouldn't get that wish if Orchid's high-pitched, gasping tone could be taken as any sort of sign.

Orchid arrived in the sunroom with a flourish. She

was all smiles and drew Alythia into a hug with kisses to spare.

"Oh, honey, it's so good to see you. How are you really?" Orchid gasped anew, her heavy perfume wafting just as powerfully as the flowing sleeves and hem of her white chiffon lounge dress.

"How are *you?*" Alythia probed carefully, studying Orchid with a narrowed and suspicious stare. "How are you doing, Ork?"

"Oh…" Orchid waved a hand. "I may be named after a flower, but I'm sturdy as a weed."

The comparison had Alythia laughing in seconds. Arm in arm, they took a few steps to take seats on a white sofa in the middle of the airy sunroom. The chair was adorned with lavender throw pillows.

"I *am* sorry for the way things turned out, Aly." Orchid had topped off Alythia's brew before she prepared a cup of the fragrant tea for herself. "I hate myself for wasting everybody's time with that damned trip."

"Oh, girl." Aly reached out to squeeze Orchid's hand. "Your heart was in the right place. You only wanted to share your happiness."

Orchid gave an unladylike snort and set the teapot back in its place atop a glazed burgundy ceramic warmer. "Aly, the marriage was a sham," she at last admitted, leaning over to draw her hair back through her fingers. "A business deal between our families." She laughed then. "I still can't believe Jayson and I were dumb enough to agree to something so antiquated. Hmph." She massaged her temples. "I guess that proves we really are too idiotic to sustain a marriage."

Aly put her teacup back on the table. "You shouldn't be so hard on yourself. You and Jay were already under a lot of stress trying to pull this off and that didn't ease up with all the other stuff goin' on between everybody else."

Orchid sucked her teeth and rolled her eyes in an obvious display of disregard for their other girlfriends. "I should've expected them to pull that bullshit."

"Ork...they didn't *pull it* on their own, you know?"

Orchid offered up another snort. "If they had behaved like ladies, the guys never would've pulled any of that stuff with them."

"Orchid..." Aly shook her head in wonder that the woman could be so obtuse. "Myrna and Jeena were damned in their eyes before they ever met Dane and Zeke. To hell with what anyone says—*reputations* are the real first impressions, whether they have merit or not."

Again Orchid rolled her eyes and then just as easily set a regretful look in place. "I only hate that you and Gage got caught up in all this and didn't have a chance to get to know each other. There were sparks flying there, right?"

"Ork—"

"Did you have time to see if there were *any* flames kickin' there?"

"We had *some* time together," Aly conceded.

Orchid looked ready to explode beneath her expectancy. "And?"

Alythia shrugged. "We're taking it slowly."

Orchid looked satisfied. "The rest of us could've learned a lot from you guys."

"Not really." Aly folded her arms across her tummy and leaned forward. "Gage and I...we moved fast, too, and I still don't know how much hell there will be to pay because of it."

"You guys looked happy, though."

Alythia couldn't deny that. "Gage Vincent is a man a woman can fall in love with very easily."

"I'm happy for you, Aly. For real." For all her good cheer however, Orchid's easy expression faded into something tight. "Makes me regret what I'm about to tell you."

Bracing herself, Alythia wondered if she was about to experience a little of the hell she'd just spoken of.

"Gage may have already told you, but I'll go on and confirm…I'm suing Jayson."

"For what?" Alythia blurted.

Orchid made a quick waving motion toward her cheek. "Have you already forgotten what happened, Aly?" She looked offended. "The fool actually had the nerve to hit me."

"And that was wrong." Alythia ventured forward carefully. "Wrong, just like the wrong you did in sleeping with one of his best friends when you were supposed to be there celebrating getting married."

Orchid came down a bit from her self-righteousness. "I regret that." Her stare faltered then.

"How in the world did it happen, Orchid? Why?" Aly turned to face her friend more fully. "Whether the marriage was a sham or not, things at least had to be going well in the bedroom. You guys were pretty…demonstrative. Or…am I mistaken?"

A sudden and uncharacteristic look of total honesty claimed Orchid Benjamin's fair-skinned face. "Sex has always been my escape, Aly." She sighed. "Pouting and wanting to get back at Mommy and Daddy for not having that chocolate waterfall at your seventeenth birthday party? Have some sex and all will be well." She shared the insight as though she were a television announcer promoting some grand new product.

"Dammit… Such an idiot." Again Orchid drew her fingers through her hair. "I guess that's what that night with Dane was about. Part of it, anyway. Some of it was me just wanting to show Myrna that she'd picked another toad and that she still hadn't found her happily-ever-after Prince Charming."

Aly leaned over to top off her tea again. "And the other part?" she asked.

"Jayson." Losing interest in maintaining perfect posture, Orchid slumped on her side of the sofa. "We had a fight about my 'friends.' That little show between Jeena and Zeke on the terrace during our group breakfast and then there was something that happened with Myrna and Dane at one of the clubs—it all pulled quite an audience. Jayson said that Clive called a little get-together with them. He told them some of the other guests had voiced concern that he allowed that sort of…element into his resort."

Alythia held the teapot but didn't pour. She was suddenly frozen to her spot. "Gage didn't say anything."

"Chances are he wouldn't." Orchid smiled sourly. "Most of the unfavorable remarks Clive's staff had received were about the women who had been causing such a ruckus."

Aly put the pot back on the warmer. She'd suddenly lost her taste for more tea.

"That's what we argued about." Orchid sat a little straighter on the sofa. "Then our *chat* led him to revealing that his family was having second thoughts about him getting tied up with someone like me. All this was even before the trip. Before we even announced the engagement. They want the Benjamin-family respect and society status but not a— How was it that he put it?" Orchid inclined her head at a thoughtful angle. "Oh, yeah, they wanted the society status but not a whoring fiancée-turned-wifey."

"Sweetie…" Aly scooted close to squeeze Orchid's hand. "I'm sorry."

"It's no big." Orchid shrugged. "I slapped him, or rather it was the big-ass bag I was carrying that delivered the blow." She smirked. "It bruised that ego of his, all right, and I guess he wanted to show me that he wasn't goin' down like Zeke. Had to hit me to show he wasn't a punk."

"Ork, do you really think suing him is the answer? Can't you just let it rest? Jay's gonna have enough on his plate dealing with the blow Dane gave him by sleeping with you."

"Hmph, Dane." Orchid's eyes narrowed a fraction. "Do you know he didn't even try to stop it? It was like he had no idea that I was about to marry his best friend. I was just another woman to bed. He was just as much the slut in all this as I was."

"Maybe that's the takeaway here." Aly leaned over and smoothed a lock of hair behind Orchid's multi-diamond-studded ear. "You're better than all this, hon. You always have been. No one *all* bad would befriend a poor nobody from the wrong side of town like me."

Orchid's eyes suddenly flashed with defiance. "You're the best person I know, Alythia Duffy." She sniffed a little as though a sob was on the horizon.

"You've helped me through some times no money can fix," she said.

Alythia cupped her cheek and smiled. "This time *you're* the only one who can fix it. Sex has been the easy way out for you. Maybe it's time for a more complex plan."

Finally, Orchid nodded. The move was slow but determined. "I'll do the heavy lifting but will you still be there for me to lean on from time to time?"

"Hmph." Aly shook her head. "Where else do you think I'd be?" She tugged her friend into a hug.

Chapter 15

In spite of the vastness of Vincent Industries and Development, Gage had created his successful enterprise using funds from a small loan he'd secured from his parents. He had refused any additional help from them and had used the money to acquire a modest five-story brick building far away from the sleek downtown high-rises and other businesses. Yet Gage had remained humble and true to his roots. He'd continued to conduct business from the simple office space that his impressive array of business associates and aspiring business associates knew to be his headquarters.

Gage hadn't remained completely averse to vanity, however. The building's top floor had been reserved as his private office, complete with a small living, dining and gaming area. The primary office space was state-of-the-art and expansive, providing the man in charge with whatever he needed to tend to his every interest.

Just then, the man in charge was mixing work and play as he took part in an overseas conference call while trying to reach the next level on the newest military-themed video game in his collection.

"I like that, Oscar. An in-person meeting sounds good," Gage agreed, all the while wincing in response to the maneuver he was attempting to complete on screen.

"Yes!" He celebrated the outcome of the risky gaming move. "We'll make it happen soon!" Gage drew the call to a close, the luster with which he completed the conversation having more to do with his satisfaction over his gaming performance than with the upcoming meeting with his associates in the U.K.

He removed the phone's headset and was gearing up for a reentry when a knock landed on his door. The exciting game was totally forgotten.

"They told me to come on up." Alythia took a tentative step just past the doorway, her uncertainty evident. "Is this a bad time?"

Slowly, Gage left the leather lounge chair where he'd taken the call. "Your timing's never bad."

"You said you'd call."

"I know." Gage maintained his spot by the chair. "Then I thought it might be better if you took the wheel on that."

She nodded. "That's what I figured."

"So what's the verdict?"

"I'm scared." Her response was simple and she accompanied it by slapping her hands to her thighs in a show of surrender. "Those feelings aren't going to go anywhere anytime soon. But I'm not ready to let all that win."

Obvious relief softening his attractive, dark face, Gage began his journey toward her. "Can I take you out now? Show everyone you're mine?"

"That sounds rather possessive, Mr. Vincent."

"You're damn right it is, Ms. Duffy." He spanned her waist, squeezing her hips. He moved on then to skim her bare skin beneath the petal-pink drop-tail blouse she wore.

"I don't know if we can be trusted out and about on Charlotte's city streets on our own, though. We may need chaperones." She sighed.

His mouth was at her neck. "What have you got in mind?" he murmured, the words holding an absent quality, as he was far more interested in ravaging the satiny flesh behind her ear.

"Dinner and maybe…some dancing…." She waited for the last to capture his attention and smiled when he raised his head to watch her expectantly. "Angela and Owen have a date night at least once a month. They'd like to share this one with us."

"I like it." He gave a singular nod and then the brilliant chocolate tone of his gaze grew heated. "I can't promise to be on my best behavior, though, even with two chaperones."

He kissed her and Aly delighted in the lazy nudging of his tongue against hers.

"What?" Gage read the weariness in her eyes when he pulled back.

Alythia pressed her lips together to gather her resolve. "I know about the meeting Clive called with you and the guys after that thing with Zeke and Jeena."

"Hell." Gage growled the curse and moved away.

"Did you think I couldn't handle knowing?" Aly followed him deeper into the office.

"It was pretty stupid." He leaned against his desk. "We were all at fault with it."

"But *we* were the unsavory element." There was no accusation in her tone.

Gage reached for her hands. "Clive's soft heart is gonna get him in some real trouble one day. He knew the sort of drama he was letting himself in for when I called and told him about Jay getting married and us wanting to take a group trip to the resort. But he's never been able to say no to a friend."

Alythia shook her head. "Well, that makes two of us since I just told Orchid I'd be her support system while she works on remodeling her character."

Gage kissed the back of her hand just as laughter burst out between them.

"Sorry for interrupting the cash flow."

Angela Hays's vibrant hazel eyes sparkled with satisfaction. She raised her wineglass to toast her little sister. "No apologies necessary, Aly-cat. In Owen's case an interrupted work flow signals free time to take his sexy wife on that Paris trip she's been hinting at."

"And the hints haven't been all that subtle." Owen Hays clinked his glass to Gage's as the two newfound friends shared a laugh.

"But that was one case I didn't mind walking away from." Owen sobered and smoothed a hand over his shaved head. "Wouldn't be good for anyone involved to follow up on it." He sent his sister-in-law an encouraging smile. "How'd you leave things with her, Aly?"

Alythia hid her hands in the bell sleeves of her emerald wrap dress. She had just told her dinner partners that Orchid might be of a mind to rethink her plans to sue her ex-fiancé. "I tried to get her to see what was right, tried to remind her that despite what anyone thinks, she *did* have a sense of right and wrong."

"Hey, now!" Owen rubbed his hands together. "That's enough to bring back my appetite."

"Oh, Lord…" Angela rolled her eyes. "Whose appetite were you using to devour that slab of flesh over there?" she said, eyeing the remaining half of the massive rib eye that Owen had ordered.

"This can wait till I take a break." Owen stood and offered a hand to his wife. "Dance with me, girl."

Angela rolled her eyes again but giggled like a small girl and didn't hesitate to accept her husband's request.

"Despite what *anyone* thinks, she did have a sense of right and wrong." Gage replayed Alythia's words when they were alone at the table. "Was that a dig at anybody in particular?"

"No." Aly pushed aside her dessert fork and rested her arms on the table. "But I do think it's fair to wonder when our feelings about our friends will get the better of us."

"Well—" Gage was pushing back from the table then too "—until we reach that point, I'll take you for a dance. Owen had the right idea."

Aly winked. "Told you he was quite a man." She took the hand Gage offered.

The music was sensuous but it kept a tempo not quite suited for the snug hold Gage kept her in.

"Your possessive streak is showing again, Mr. Vincent."

"Good. I guess that means I've achieved my goal." His hand firmed at the small of her back and he drew her into a kiss that grew deeper with each second that passed.

Aly was first to regain consciousness of their surroundings. She tugged at his tie until he freed her mouth.

"So what's showing your possessive streak supposed to achieve?"

"It's supposed to remind me that it's past time for me to get you out of here and into someplace with more privacy."

"We haven't even had dessert yet, you know?" She bit her lip on a smile.

"Well, well, Ms. Duffy." He began to gnaw at her neck. "You're so very right about that," he muttered.

Alythia took a detour toward the ladies' room when she and Gage left the dance floor. She was touching up her lipstick when a familiar voice caught her ear.

"Well...well, they say the quiet ones are usually the freakiest."

"Mur!" Aly called, whirling from the mirror and happy to find her friend standing just inside the bathroom.

"I see one of us came back with a man." The remark could have been considered playful were it not for the distinct look of reproach in Myrna's alluring eyes.

"Mur...don't." Aly raised a hand wearily. "Can't we just put all that petty stuff that happened in Anegada behind us?"

"That's sweet." Myrna folded her arms across the

square bodice of the black baby-doll dress that flattered her long legs. "And it's easier for some than others."

"Honey, Dane—Dane wasn't worth it. Orchid said that he had no qualms about sleeping with her and that he didn't think twice about what she had going on with Jayson."

"Oh, please! Like she cared!" Myrna stalked about on the open-toed stilettos she wore. "The only thing she probably gave him time to tell her was where his bed was."

"Myrna, stop." Alythia slashed the air with a wave of her hand when she ventured forward. "We've been friends too damn long. Too much is invested in us for you to let some snake like Dane Spears ruin it."

"Oh, Dane didn't *ruin* us, Aly. Our weird friendship has been circling the bowl for years." She gave Alythia a judgmental once-over. "You don't even want to associate with us, always using business as an excuse to get out of spending time with us." She suddenly smiled. "But then again, I guess it was all worth it. I hear congrats are in order."

Aly frowned. "What are you talking about?"

"I guess all that private time you want everyone to think you weren't giving to one of the most powerful men in town paid off. Seems you're one of the lucky bastards about to grab digs in that swanky new downtown high-rise of his."

Alythia stilled noticeably. "How do you know that?"

Myrna slowly threw up her hands. "Aly, please… you're not the only one with powerful friends, or bed partners, I guess I should say…." She regarded Aly more closely then. "Whoa…you didn't know you were in, did you? How interesting. I wonder why that is? Why hasn't that cutie of yours told you what I'm sure you've been waiting to hear for months?"

Myrna paced the outer area of the powder room, tapping a finger to her chin and presenting herself as a study in concentration. "Maybe he knows you were just screwing him for the building. Though that's no hardship, as gorgeous as he is. Guess he just wants to…milk you a little longer before he gives you the good news and your walking papers."

Alythia blinked, assessing the new information.

Myrna's apologetic look was belied by a triumphant smile. "Forgive me, Aly. I'm not trying to hurt you, girl." She shrugged and headed for the door. "You were a good friend, but you should be prepared for little run-ins like this, especially if you plan on holding to the claim that you would've gotten that space if you *hadn't* upped the ante on your bid." She winked and pulled open the powder room door. "Enjoy your dinner. Owen and Angela look great."

Then she was gone. Aly returned to studying her mirrored reflection.

The couples said their good-nights shortly after dessert. Alythia had enjoyed the entire evening in spite of her "toilet talk" with Myrna. Part of her mourned the loss of such an old friendship. Though it *was* indeed a lost friendship. She could accept that. Myrna was angry over a lot more than her, and it would take a very long time for her to come back around.

Still, another part of her was wickedly peeved, but at Myrna or herself Alythia couldn't be completely certain.

She was so absorbed in her thoughts, in fact, that

she didn't realize they were parked outside her complex until Gage was at the passenger side of his truck and freeing her from the seat belt.

She blinked and was suddenly all smiles. "What a great night, huh?" She took the hand he offered and stepped out of the car.

"Owen and Angela are so much fun to hang out with. Thanks for coming with me...." Alythia rambled on so much that she didn't take much notice of Gage's extreme silence.

They headed into her downtown apartment building and covered the ten-flight elevator ride to her floor.

"Can I get you anything?" Aly offered once they were inside the apartment and she had tossed aside her things en route to the kitchen.

"You can tell me what Myrna wanted."

Alythia stopped short, turning and frowning a bit when she discovered that he hadn't left the foyer. Gage was still resting back on the front door, hands hidden in the deep pockets of his trousers. Alythia retraced her steps, her expression screaming a question she couldn't form the words to ask.

Gage read it easily enough and shrugged. "I saw her at the restaurant, figured she'd find a way to get time alone with you."

"She came to congratulate me." Aly smiled dourly at the question coming to his handsome face and continued. "Seems I've been accepted into the new downtown space." She ducked her head, fiddling with the edge of one of the wrist-hugging sleeves of her wrap dress. "Were you going to tell me, Gage?" She kept her head down.

"No." His answer was simply stated and he took her

by the wrist before she could move away from him. "And I'm leaning toward us having a 'do not discuss' clause in all matters having to do with our businesses."

"A 'do not discuss' clause." Aly ignored her desire to smile. "I don't think I've ever heard of one of those before."

"Good, 'cause I just came up with it." He raised a broad shoulder, letting it slide up along the door where he still reclined. "I'm known for being innovative like that."

"Well, it's definitely that." She didn't resist leaning in when he tugged.

Gage made no effort to relinquish his stance against the door. He had a strong hold on her wrist, and his hand at her neck cradled her there with a gentleness. His kiss was a subtle cross between commanding and cajoling. Soon Aly's fingers were entwined about the fabric of his jacket lapels, tiny moans escaping her as she took what he gave and reciprocated with her own brand of passion.

With a pat to her cheek, Gage withdrew from the kiss but remained near. He studied her face, searching her bright eyes with a measuring fire. "You aren't gonna do something crazy like refuse to take the space, are you?" He rested his head back against the door. "I'll break my own rule this time and tell you that I left all of the decision making to my assistant and the rest of the team. Until you told me, I had no idea you were even connected to the bid pool."

"Thank you. And no, I'm not going to back out of accepting the space." She shook her head when he gave her a mock look of surprise. "I've wanted a more upscale location for a long time and that was before I even knew you or knew that you were connected to it all."

"So we're okay?" He pulled her closer into him.

Alythia curved her hands about his tie. "We're okay."

His sigh held a melodramatic flavor. "I'm sorry, but I'm gonna need more than your word on that, Ms. Duffy."

"More? What more do I have to give?" She played innocent with relish.

The liquid-chocolate intensity of his stare harbored a more molten quality when it traveled the length of her. "You ask the best questions." His lips closed on her earlobe, where he barely suckled.

The move was hypnotic and so much so that Alythia didn't even realize he'd located the ties and fastenings of her wrap dress until she felt the rush of cool air against her bare skin. The front of the chic dress hung open to reveal the lacy emerald-colored bra-and-panties ensemble she wore underneath.

Gage's branding touch spanned her waist, curving around to provide a cradle to her bottom as he lifted her off her feet. Aly didn't care where he took her so long as he didn't let her go. She let her nose trail the line of his jaw and the side of his neck adorned by the cologne he wore.

She was jolted suddenly by the cool wood beneath her bare bottom. The sensation roused a gasp from her lips. She realized he'd somehow removed her panties on the way to the high message table in the foyer where he'd placed her.

Aly needed but a moment to acclimate herself to her new position. She let Gage brush the dress from her shoulders while she worked to relieve him of his own clothing. As usual, he was more intent on having her naked first. He gave playful slaps to her hands when they got in the way of him achieving that. Alythia, however, was too determined to have him as bare as he wanted her. When he slapped at her hand, she retaliated with a slap to his and fixed him with a bold, saucy smile when he chuckled his surprise.

Eventually they met on common ground, both gloriously nude and hungry for the sensual friction their bodies provided when they made contact. Gage braced suddenly weakened hands on the message desk. His long legs had gone rubbery beneath Alythia's attention. She was hungrily suckling his earlobe and emitting soft feminine sounds of desire that stirred his arousal and ego as deliciously as her thumbs stroked his nipples.

When she let her mouth cascade over the rippling dark-coffee pecs of his stunning chest, he rested his forehead to the crook of her shoulder. He shuddered when she began a merciless assault on his nipples with her lips and tongue, while her hand closed over his sex and began working him with erotic fervor.

"You're killin' me…." he moaned.

Aly smiled and brushed her thumb across the tip of his erection. "I don't think so," she mused.

"Alythia…please…"

She shivered, wanting very much to extend that particular plan of foreplay, loving the power of driving such a man out of his mind. Still, she was just as much a slave to her own needs and wanted him inside her just as much as he wanted to be there.

Gage had already taken a condom from a well-stocked jacket pocket before Alythia had unceremoniously tugged the garment from his shoulders and let it fall to the floor. Now the item lay on the message desk and Aly fumbled feverishly for it.

He had hardly given her time to fully secure their protection when once again his hands were cupping her bottom. Focus unwavering, he positioned her as deftly as Aly guided him toward her core. Gasps and groans colored the foyer simultaneously. The volume of the fevered sounds heightened with every vigorous thrust from Gage or wicked twist of the hips from Alythia. The table added its own groans to the melee, creaking in protest of them enjoying one another so freely, inhibitions be damned.

Gage finally took Aly off the table and held her to the wall, without ever breaking his connection to her. To ensure that, Aly locked her legs at his lean waist, her sensation cresting at the feel of him stretching her intimate walls and the delight of her bare nipples grazing his.

Their moves had carried them to the doorway of the living room. Aly cursed the relentless press of the framework into her back but she wasn't about to complain. It was of little importance; Gage had already grown tired of that venue and was depositing Alythia on the back of her sofa moments later. Still they were intimately connected and Aly luxuriated in both the soothing cushions beneath her bottom and his exploration of her body. He held her thighs apart, preventing her from locking her legs about his waist. Instead, he wanted to penetrate, to mark her as deeply as he could.

There was nothing Gage needed to prove to himself. She was his. Yet he wanted to leave no doubts of that in her mind. That night was to be about him giving her his all. The thought had a shattering effect and he was then releasing himself inside the condom's thin sheet far more quickly than he had intended. He gnawed her cheek and shoulder, patting her bottom and loving the feel of her continuous clutch and release of his shaft.

"Alythia?" He felt himself refueling for another round and the need for additional protection was in order.

"Mmm…?"

"Where's my jacket?"

"What?" Gage probed when he heard the short laugh Alythia gave in to her coffee the next morning in her small kitchen.

"You're not an easy man to figure out." She smiled.

"In what way?" He looked playfully insulted. "I thought I laid myself pretty bare last night."

"I'll say." She sipped of her coffee and then cradled the mug between her hands. "One day you're commanding the head of a table on board a lavish jet and the next you're here having bacon and eggs in my little kitchen."

"And they're damn good eggs, too." Brows raised, he was already leaning over the table to help himself to more of the fluffy scramble. He took note of her expression and suddenly feigned uncertainty.

"Should I be down on your cooking or complaining over the cramped dining space?"

"No…and thanks for being so considerate. I can definitely do without the colorful commentary about my residence."

"Good, because I really want us to have dinner here tonight." Gage cleaned his plate of the second helping of eggs. "Since you took care of breakfast, I'll handle dinner."

"You? Cook?"

Gage shook his head. "I said I'd *handle* dinner—never said I'd cook it."

"That's too bad." Alythia set her amethyst gaze to appraising his torso, hidden by a partially buttoned shirt. "Nothing sexier than a man who cooks."

"Does Owen cook?"

Aly laughed. "That's one of the few things he prefers to leave to Angela. He only visits the kitchen to eat."

"I see. In that case, I'll put cooking lessons on the list ASAP."

"No need." Aly propped her bare feet on the unoccupied chair at the small round table they shared. "There *are* other places to be talented besides the kitchen, you know?"

"Hmm… You may be right." Gage tapped his chin, finished off the rest of his juice, wiped his mouth and hands, and then stood.

Alythia accepted the hand he offered and the kiss that followed.

"Walk me out?" He made the request as his sensuous exploration of her mouth continued.

Eventually, cooler heads prevailed over hormones. Arm in arm, Gage and Alythia made their way to the front door.

"I'll see you for dinner." He patted the bare hint of cheek visible at the hem of the sleep T-shirt she still wore and indulged in another quick plundering of her mouth. Then he left.

Aly watched him go, waving him on down the hall when he pivoted to return to her door. As he disappeared down the hall, Aly thought about how used to this she could become.

"Head out of the clouds, Aly...." she whispered, and headed back to the kitchen to clean up from breakfast. The kettle continued to simmer on the stove, sending its sounds of steaming water into the air. Additionally, there was the dull drone of the television newscaster delivering the morning forecast and traffic conditions.

Alythia only barely paid attention to the voices as she wiped down the table and loaded the dishwasher. Soon, though, she was riveted to the television screen, having done a double take when she saw footage of Orchid leaving some arts event she'd attended earlier in the year. Beneath the footage, a caption read Local Heiress Sues Former Fiancé.

Slowly, Alythia settled in one of the dining table chairs and mourned her friend's decision. She set her forehead against her palm when the newscaster added that prominent Charlotte attorney Owen Hays would be arguing Ms. Benjamin's case.

Alythia was massaging her temples when the doorbell rang. She wondered if it was at all possible to fake not being at home. But the fact that it may have been Gage was enough to get her out of the chair. While she would've loved to forget everything and fall into his arms for the rest of the day and night, she knew that probably wouldn't happen for a while. Aly cursed the fact that she and Gage were once again on the cusp of another friendship melodrama.

At the door, Aly gave in to a significant measure of relief. Marianne, not Gage, stood on the other side of the door.

"Mari, hey—"

Marianne moved fast past her before Alythia could give her a proper greeting. Mari kept hold of Aly's upper arms while pushing her into the foyer.

"We may have a problem," she said.

Chapter 16

News of *Benjamin v. Muns* had reached Gage by the time he'd arrived at his office building. He'd stopped off at his condo for a change of clothes, regretting that he hadn't checked the news before leaving. His staff, however, had wasted no time informing him of the brewing storm or the fact that he already had guests waiting in his office.

Gage didn't need to ask. Since he'd just left Alythia, there were only three other people his staff was under clear orders to grant immediate access.

At the elevator he hesitated. He very much wanted to return to his truck and heavily contemplated going back to Alythia's. Foregoing his wants, he moved onward and before he knew it, he was seated behind his desk. There he looked out over the stony faces of his friends as they recovered from the shock he'd just given them.

"What the hell do you mean you won't back Jay on this, G?" Dane was first to recover from his surprise.

"I don't think I was unclear." Gage's expression harbored a stoniness surpassed only by the grimness of his voice. Without waiting on another reply from Dane, he turned his next words to Jayson Muns.

"We go way back, Jay."

"All the way back," Jayson confirmed with a brief nod.

Gage returned the gesture. "I'll help you however I can while you deal with this thing but I stand by what I just said. I draw the line at sitting up in a courtroom with you as part of this wall of support Dane's talkin' about."

"G, that's bull—" Dane began.

"And how the hell are *you* offering support to Jay when you're responsible for all this?" Gage interjected.

"Aw, Gage, please! How long we had each other's backs? Jay knew I was just lookin' out for him."

"Lookin' out?" Gage felt as though he was on the verge of laughter.

"I meant to show him what that wench was really like." Dane planted a fist to the center of his chest as though giving credence to his plan. "She didn't need much coaxing, hardly any. What the hell kind of wife would she have made for our boy?"

"How'd you get him to buy that crap?" Gage's tone was incredulous, his eyes narrowed with blatant disbelief.

Dane's lips curled on the beginnings of a snarl. "I didn't have to get him to *buy* a damn thing. He already knew it was true. Everybody in town knows what Or-

chid Benjamin is behind all that money and family respect."

"Jay—" Gage turned back to Jayson, having silently
acknowledged that Dane Spears was blind to everything
except his own self-importance and opinion "—you *did*
hit the woman. Don't forget that. What D's suggesting
makes it look like we all approve."

"And that would be wrong, G," Dane chimed in before Jay could summon a reply. "It would be wrong if
it wasn't for the fact that Jay was protecting himself."

Gage did laugh then. "You're not suggesting that he
claim this was all self-defense?"

"G? She *did* hit me first. That's the truth of it," Jay
said matter-of-factly. "She hit me and I—I reacted.
Granted, not in the best way, but after what happened
with Zeke and Jeena, I wasn't taking a chance with the
woman's violent streak."

"That's gonna be your statement for the press, Jay?"
Gage set his elbow on the arm of the desk chair and
massaged the bridge of his nose. "Please don't tell me
you're bringing that into evidence." He shook his head
when there was no response from Jayson. "If you are,"
he continued, "you should know that Alythia's brother-
in-law is no slouch in the courtroom." He fixed Jay with
unmasked sympathy.

"You better hope Owen Hays doesn't present wit-
nesses from that little spat. Even though Jeena was at
fault, Hays will find all the other folks who were there
and saw the three of us trying to hold Zeke down from
going after her. They'll try to make it look like we're a
bunch of woman beaters if we sit there and back you in
this. I want to support you, man, but that sort of com-

parison doesn't sit well with me." Gage let his thoughts rest on Alythia.

"That's it, isn't it?" Dane was apparently thinking of Aly, as well. "You don't want to stick by a friend you've known since forever, because you don't want to upset your latest piece of candy?"

"D—"

"And a delicious piece she is." Dane barreled ahead over Gage. "Not that I've had the pleasure of sampling—"

"Dane, man, easy," Zeke said, having seen the murderous narrowing of Gage's eyes and the clench of his fists.

Dane, however, had found a line to tug. "It's cool, Zeke, it's cool. Gage here just needs to ask himself if he really, *really* thinks *Alythia* is any better than the rest of her friends, who are skanks."

Gage stood, crashing his chair into the credenza that spanned the length of his desk. Zeke and Jayson came to their feet, as well, ready to separate their friends if the meeting turned physical.

"Gage!"

Webb Reese burst into the office then. Desperation had overridden all sense of decorum as he interrupted the goings-on between the four tense men in the room.

"Was she worth it, man?" Dane roared, waving a hand toward Webb.

"Webb?" Gage didn't miss the guilt flash on his assistant's face.

"Is that how Ms. Duffy got her new downtown digs, Webb?" Dane was smug and shrugged at Gage. "Guess your right-hand man is gonna try keeping it all quiet a little longer. Trust me, man, no one's gonna hear a peep out of me." He turned to Webb. "At least be honest with your boss. You know he's been good to you. Tell him how Alythia Duffy's right hand girl gave up the panties to close the deal."

Webb shook his head wildly and spread his hands. "Gage, I swear, it wasn't like that."

"I swear it wasn't like that." Marianne spread her hands in a supplicating fashion across the nook counter.

Alythia squeezed Marianne's hands and gave them a tug. "*I* believe you, but you know it won't be hard for someone to make it look like you slept with Webb to give me a leg up on the bid…pun intended." She smiled sympathetically when Mari put her forehead on the counter.

"But I didn't even sleep with him," Mari moaned. "We didn't even go out together."

"I— Huh?" Aly tapped her fingers to her brow.

"I never even talked to Webb Reese before the day Gage asked him to call and help him find you. Sounds like Gage didn't have any way to contact you."

"No." Aly picked at the microscopic balls of lint that clung to the worn sweatpants she'd thrown on when Marianne arrived. "The trip to Anegada wasn't about matchmaking." She smirked. "At least, we were all stupid enough to believe it wasn't. We were going to celebrate our friends' wedding. Anyway, no numbers or emails were exchanged."

"Well, I told him I couldn't help. I didn't even know the guy. No way was I giving contact info on one of my clients." Marianne finally helped herself to the piping-hot herbal tea Aly had served her.

"So he—Webb—tells me that one of the sales associates at the boutique suggested he give me a call. I think he even got your cell number and shared it with Gage, but I guess you didn't answer."

"And then he showed up on my doorstep in Aspen." Marianne cringed. "Sorry."

"Don't be." Alythia didn't try to hide her contentment and hugged herself. "It was the best time of my life."

"I'm glad." Marianne bent her head to shield her face with tousles of her reddish hair. "Even so, I told Webb that I couldn't just give your info to someone I didn't know and then he dropped Gage's name and I..." She sent Aly a resigned look.

"I really am so sorry about this, Aly. Hmph, an apology is why Webb called." Marianne tugged at the tassels of her white sweatshirt. "He said he was sorry for upsetting me when he called. I told him it was fine but he said he wanted to take me out and make it up but I didn't think it was a good idea." She burst into quick laughter.

"So of course I run into him at Rooney's." She cited a cigar bar that was popular with the business crowd after hours.

"We were both there." Marianne put her head in her hands. "He was there with someone I knew and they introduced us. Afterward we stayed a little longer, had a few drinks..."

"Nice..." Aly reached over to help herself to Marianne's tea.

"Aly, I promise it didn't go any further than that. We talked about our jobs, but the conversation *never* brushed up against our clients or our clients' business. I know I'm probably making a mountain out of my molehill of a dating life." She brought her elbow to the counter and propped her chin on her fist. "I just thought you should know."

"I appreciate it." Aly massaged her nape. "It's amazing how many molehills have brushed up against me and Gage's relationship in the short time we've known each other."

"So...we're good?" Mari cringed again.

Aly squeezed her hands and nodded. "We're good. You're fine."

Marianne's expression harbored a trace of uncertainty. "And what are *you* gonna do?"

Aly made her way around the breakfast nook. "Guess it's time to face another round of music. I can only hope this is the last movement."

"Something tells me I've really come at a bad time." Alythia stood in the doorway of Gage's office and observed what looked to be a war zone.

His expression gave away nothing when he stood from the heap of books and picture frames. "What makes you say that?"

"Just a lucky guess." She hooked the strap of her purse over the office doorknob and tentatively ventured deeper inside the room. "Have you seen the news?" she asked.

"You're referring to the trial of the decade?" Gage tossed a scant glance toward the wreckage on the floor and grinned. "Yeah, I heard. I heard a lot today."

"Did it have anything to do with the tornado that swept your office?"

Gage tossed the picture frame he carried back to the mess on the floor. "Dane wants to get a support group together for Jay. Wants all of us to rally together and sit in his corner at the hearing."

Alythia couldn't help it. She laughed.

Gage's sour expression showed signs of improvement and he smiled.

"Are you serious?"

Gage shrugged. "Sadly, yes." He kicked at some of the wreckage.

"Men are strange." Aly shook her head and brushed off a bit of debris from one of the chairs before the desk and took a seat there. "So quick you are to forgive the betrayals of your boyhood friends."

Gage took his turn at bursting into laughter then. "You're very mistaken, Ms. Duffy, so let me school you. Men like that are few and far between." He laughed again, but the humor fueling it had curbed considerably.

"I'm starting to think that my old friend Jay doesn't have as much going on upstairs as he used to."

The duo indulged in more laughter. Unfortunately, the good vibes spent themselves far too soon.

"So is that what led to this recent redecoration of your office?" Aly scanned the room again.

Sighing, Gage took a seat on the corner of his desk and seemed to be weighing his response. "The 'redecoration' happened after my assistant, Webb Reese, came to tell me about his date with your business manager— Marianne?"

Aly only nodded as more of the pieces began to fall in place.

"Somehow Dane knew about it already. He got vocal over it. Things got ugly."

"Gage." Aly scooted to the edge of her chair, his explanation motivating her into a vocal spree of her own.

"Whatever Dane said, it—it wasn't like that. Marianne says she and Webb, it was all just by chance—"

"Alythia—"

"They met at a cigar bar. They didn't even *meet* there, just happened to be there at the same time and—"

"Alythia, stop."

The underlying thickness of his voice caught her attention and she obeyed. Her heart sank as she acknowledged that he'd finally had enough.

"Guess you're sick of this, huh?" Nervously, she fingered the pleats of her skirt.

Gage massaged his forehead. "You have no idea how much…and I think it'll all get worse before it gets any better."

"Yeah…" She bowed her head, unable to look at him. She raised it quickly, however, at his next words.

"I think I'm falling in love with you, Alythia Duffy, and I'm sick of just *thinking* it—I'm ready to know it."

Aly expelled the breath she hadn't realized she'd been holding. "I think I'm falling in love with you, too. But our…attempts at getting to the *knowing* stage haven't been too successful, have they?"

Gage left the desk and pulled Alythia to her feet. "Say that again." He cupped her face, brushing at both her cheeks with his thumbs.

She smiled, not at all confused by his command. "I think I'm falling in love with you, too."

His kiss was quick yet deep and probing in its brevity. Afterward he held his forehead to hers.

"I can't accept what Jay did but as a friend I can't turn my back on him. Can you understand that?"

She nodded. "If you can understand that I'll need to

be a friend to Orchid or Jeena if Zeke decides to come after *her*."

Weak albeit easy laughter hummed between them then.

"One trial at a time, all right?" Gage pleaded.

"We're a couple of saps, you know?"

"And still our friends depend on us...." Gage murmured, skimming his lips along her temple.

"That's because they all know we won't turn our backs on them."

Gage returned to the desk and took a seat, keeping Alythia standing before him. "Too many years, too many memories, I guess." He planted a kiss to the centers of her palms.

"You think we can handle what's coming?" Aly linked her arms about his neck.

"I trust us." He drew her down, nuzzling her ear. "I think we could use some rejuvenation time before we head back into the storm, though."

"Just what did you have in mind?" She leaned back as far as he would let her.

"I was thinking about this little place called Anegada." Gage sighed and tugged Alythia back into the sweetest kiss.

* * * * *

REQUEST YOUR FREE BOOKS!

2 FREE NOVELS
PLUS 2 FREE GIFTS!

KIMANI™ ROMANCE

Love's ultimate destination!